CW00417946

Divining the Dead

Jo Wolfe psychic detective

Book 2

Wendy Cartmell

This edition published 2020
Costa Press

ISBN: 9798627483283

By Wendy Cartmell

Sgt Major Crane crime thrillers
Deadly Steps
Deadly Nights
Deadly Honour
Deadly Lies
Deadly Widow
Hijack
Deadly Cut
Deadly Proof

Emma Harrison Mysteries
Past Judgement
Mortal Judgement
Joint Judgement

Crane and Anderson crime thrillers
Death Rites
Death Elements
Death Call
A Grave Death
A Cold Death

Supernatural Mysteries
Gamble with Death
Touching the Dead
Divining the Dead

For Ben
whose unusual gift inspired this series.
Thank you!

.

1

Sebastian Trulove approached the Italian restaurant, the bright lights spilling onto the pavement in the central shopping area of Chichester. He grinned. He loved it when a plan came together. There should be two things waiting for him inside; one was his wife, and the other, much more importantly, would be a briefcase. His wife, Miranda, wasn't what people would call a soul mate, rather a trophy. A stunningly beautiful woman, but rather lacking in intellect. He loved her in his own way. But he much preferred money. Or the company of his friends, or of a rather special friend.

Anyway, the trouble was that being a member of parliament wasn't terribly well paid. Or at least not well paid enough to keep Truelove in the manner he would like to become accustomed. So he'd hit on a plan to use his influence to help those who had rather more than he had and were willing to spread it around. This time, all it had taken was a word in the right ear and a briefcase full of money would soon be his. He'd arranged to have it left at the restaurant, by Odin. Sebastian knew little of Odin, only that he represented a consortium of developers who needed planning permission to build a new out of town shopping centre, and that they were willing to pay handsomely for said permission. He and Odin had become close during their dealings, but in truth Truelove knew little about his new friend. They'd agreed that their friendship should be kept in the shadows. It was either that or lose Odin and the money. Truelove had declared he was unable to do either.

Sebastian strode towards the door, his sharp business suit covered by a camel-coloured coat, the tan leather shoes he wore matching it. He threw away the burning end of a small cheroot and pulled open the restaurant door. He knew the maître d' well and made a beeline for him. Stood behind his reception desk, the small man looked up and recognised the MP immediately.

'Good evening, Mr Trulove, welcome.'

'Matteo,' acknowledged Sebastian. He doubted that was really the man's name, but it sounded authentically Italian and that was all that mattered. His slicked-backed, black hair and small moustache added to the illusion.

'Your wife is waiting at your table,' Matteo said.

But Sebastian wasn't much interested in her. 'I believe you have something for me?'

'Indeed, Mr Trulove,' and Matteo pulled out a briefcase from underneath the desk. 'Do you want me to keep it here for you?'

'No, thank you, I'll take it with me to the table.'

'Very well,' and Matteo handed over the precious case.

The moment it was in his hands, Sebastian sighed. At last. Inside were many thousands of pounds that would soon find their way to his safety deposit box in a local bank. After giving Matteo his coat, Sebastian weaved through the full tables to his waiting wife. The restaurant was as popular as ever, he noticed. Kissing Miranda on the cheek, he placed the briefcase under the table and sat opposite her. He'd check the contents of the case later, in the privacy of his study at home.

'Wine?' his wife asked.

'Prosecco,' Trulove said. 'The best they have. I feel like celebrating.'

2

DI Jo Wolfe was late. Glancing at her watch she swore. How had she managed to be 30 minutes behind schedule? It was all her bloody father's fault. A retired-police detective inspector, he was always keen to catch up on his daughter's cases. But they'd spent too long chatting about the success of her last one, and so she was late to the team's celebratory meal.

Jo could see the Italian restaurant a little further up the street. Her footsteps echoed off the silent buildings. Shops locked up tightly followed her progress with blank eyes, sending a shiver down her back. She kept up a quick pace, until she could see the team sat at a table in the window. They weren't eating yet, thank goodness. They must have waited for her.

As she watched them, a shadow raced across the brightly lit windows. Jo turned as her scalp began to prickle, but there was no one there. Chichester city centre was a pedestrian area, so the shadow couldn't have been from a car driving past. She shook her head to chase away her sudden… what? Premonition? Feeling of foreboding?

DS Byrd saw her and raised his glass. Jo pushed away the bad vibe she'd just felt. It was nothing and her eyes locked with Byrd's. Their budding relationship was the best thing that had happened to her in a long time. He had been there to save her from the killer they'd dubbed Anubis, after the Egyptian God of Death and had hardly left her side since. She smiled at him and raised her hand, returning his greeting. There was an empty chair opposite him, obviously for her. The rest of her small core team were already there, Judith her office manager, Bill, their forensic specialist, DC Jill Sandy and Jeremy, their favourite pathologist. She was the only one missing.

She took a step towards the restaurant.

She never made it to the door.

The explosion stopped her in her tracks.

The bang echoed off the shops and buildings. Bouncing. Ear bursting. The loudest noise she'd ever heard.

First the front of the restaurant disintegrated. Then it felt as if all the air had been sucked out of the immediate area.

She couldn't breathe or speak. Nor could she hear anything. It was as though she were in a vacuum. All Jo could do was open her mouth in shock. There were no words to describe how she felt about what had just happened.

Her team. Gone.

Byrd. Gone.

Gradually her hearing came back and she could hear the tinkling of glass as it fell around her. It landed in her hair and on her clothes. Lethal snow. It was everywhere. There was a cacophony of screams from building alarms. Then came the sirens. No doubt police, ambulances and fire engines.

Someone was screaming. She realised it was her.

The blast had blown her off her feet. She got up slowly. Her hands and knees were cut, but she ignored the pain and the blood. All she could see was the gaping hole that was the front of the restaurant.

Where her team had sat.

Where Byrd had been.

3

Eddie Byrd slowly came round, wondering what the hell had just happened. One minute he was drinking from his glass of wine and watching Jo approach the restaurant. And the next he appeared to be on his back on the floor. Looking around he realised the restaurant was now a place of carnage. It was unrecognisable. A minute ago they'd been looking forward to a hearty Italian meal. Now? Well now the room didn't resemble a restaurant, it was more like a war zone. The sort of buildings that were shown on television, pictures from far flung places like Syria. Surely stuff like that didn't happen in sleepy Chichester. But it appeared it did.

He tried to move, but his legs were pinned under something large and heavy. Concrete? A steel beam? Then he realised it must be the table.

There seemed to have been some sort of explosion. More than likely a bomb, he decided. The lights had been blown out, but he could make out shadows and pockets that were lit from the remaining lights in the street and fires in the restaurant. He began to feel around him but couldn't touch anyone else. Where the hell were the rest of the team? Then a thought hit him. Jo. Where the hell was Jo? He'd seen her walking towards him, outside in the street. They'd waived. Then nothing.

'JO!' he screamed. 'JO!'

In the distance he heard sirens, relieved to know help was coming. It wouldn't be long before the emergency services arrived. But he hadn't heard a reply to his call. His shallow breathing quickened. Fear gripped his heart and wouldn't let go. He couldn't lose her. Not now. Not after she'd been through so much at the hands of Anubis. Not after he'd finally managed to break through the protective ice encasing her heart. It wasn't fair.

He was hyperventilating.

He tried to calm himself. Deliberately took long, slow breaths. Panicking wouldn't help his situation, only hinder it.

He took a deep breath. It didn't help. Panic returned. 'JO!' he screamed. 'JO!'

4

The dead were screaming. The only person who could hear them was Jo.

She couldn't make out what they were saying, so she listened for a voice she knew so well. Byrd.

She couldn't hear him.

She could breathe again.

But what about the rest of the team? Again she tried to separate the voices, concentrating on each one in turn.

Nothing. She didn't recognise any of them.

She tried to turn away from the dead. It was time to focus on the living. But they wouldn't be silenced. It was like a bad case of tinnitus, a whistling sound in the background. But they weren't whistling. They were screaming.

Police cars arrived, rocketing up the pedestrianised streets, parking so their headlights shone on the front of the restaurant. Jo shielded her eyes until they adjusted.

An officer approached Jo. 'Are you alright? Are you hurt?' he shouted over the alarms.

Jo felt in her coat pocket and produced her ID. Looking at it with the aid of a small torch, he said, 'Do you know what happened, Ma'am?'

Jo forgave him for using the usual greeting for a female

superior officer, although she hated the moniker with a vengeance. 'Looks like a bomb. Five members of my team are inside, I need to go and find them.'

She pocketed her ID and moved past him. As Jo stepped over the rubble, which was all that remained of the front of the restaurant, she heard moans.

'BYRD,' she shouted. 'CAN YOU HEAR ME?'

'Jo,' came a weak voice from somewhere near her feet. 'Jo. Help.'

She fell to her knees and shining the torch app on her phone in the general direction of the voice, she found him. He was pinned under a large table, lying on a bed of broken glass and crockery, with what looked like pasta in his hair and sauce splattered across his face. She hoped it was sauce. Not blood.

Jo wasn't sure whether to laugh or cry, so she did a bit of both, glad that no one could see her display of emotion, apart from Byrd.

5

As more people arrived to help, Jo moved out of the way so the fire brigade could rescue her trapped team. Several burly men picked up the heavy table, carrying it outside, careful not to tread on those underneath it.

As the firemen moved away, their places were taken by paramedics. With their lips close to ears, they ascertained how each victim was feeling, which part of their body hurt and making decisions as to who could be moved. The walking wounded were helped to waiting ambulances. Following Byrd, she found he was in pretty good shape. His legs hurt but he didn't think they were broken. His ribs were sore, but again he thought it was just bruising. He wanted to stay behind with her, but the paramedics were insisting that he go to hospital.

'Go on, Byrd, you know it makes sense. You're suffering from shock if nothing else. I couldn't bear it if there's an internal injury we know nothing about, with fatal consequences. So behave yourself and do as you're told!'

'Yes, Boss,' he grinned, giving her a mock salute. But he did as he was told without any further protest, but not before stealing a kiss.

Jo watched Byrd's ambulance drive away, her lips still tingling from his kiss. The thought that Byrd was alright and would soon be by her side again gave her the courage and determination to carry on. She was confident that Byrd was OK as he'd been furthest away from the blast. The others, Bill, Jill and Jeremy, were also suffering from shock and bruising, so should recover quickly. But it was Judith she was most concerned about. Sat at the top of the table, she had been closest to the blast. Her back and arms were burned and the medics were concerned about her breathing. They were afraid she'd inhaled too much hot air from the explosion and smoke from the subsequent fires. They would be monitoring her closely. For now, she was lying, face down, in the back of an ambulance, hooked up to oxygen.

As the ambulances screamed away, Jo turned to see DCI Crooks walking towards her.

'This is a bloody mess,' he said by way of greeting.

'It certainly is, Guv,' Jo agreed.

'How are the team?'

'Good,' she said, hoping to God they were. 'Looks like just shock and bruising, although Judith has some burns. Byrd, Sandy, Jeremy and Bill are on their way to hospital. They wanted to stay but need to be checked over before being allowed back to help.'

Jeremy Grogan and Bill Burke were highly committed and had wanted to stay on site, which was commendable but potentially dangerous. A scene such as this required careful, painstaking handling of evidence. Nothing must be allowed to risk that, by the use of injured colleagues, which could result in vital evidence being thrown out by the defence should there be any subsequent prosecutions.

Crooks nodded, 'That's a relief. I'm off to see the Gold Commander, phone if you need me.'

'Yes, Sir.'

On a major incident such as this, normal police procedure was to appoint a Gold Commander to take overall control of the troops and ensure the safety of the public. An awesome responsibility that Jo had no wish to aspire to. She turned back to look at the ruins of the restaurant. It was time to pick her way to the seat of the blast and to listen to those clamouring to tell her what had happened to them. But first she had better phone her dad and let him know she was safe.

6

After calling her father, Jo realised that she was turning away from touching the dead, because of fear. She knew that the moment she stepped back into the scene of the tragedy the voices would start. And it wouldn't be pleasant. It would be heart breaking. It was an awesome responsibility that Jo carried on her shoulders. The dead deserved to be heard. She couldn't let them down.

After gulping in air that tasted of acrid smoke, she stepped back into the restaurant, walking across the space left by her team. She didn't have to go any further into the room. She didn't have to find any bodies to touch. The dead assaulted her, recognising someone they could communicate with. It wasn't surprising. Firstly the shock for them would have been severe. One minute a person was sitting in a popular restaurant, looking forward to a meal. The next they were dead. It just didn't compute. And who could blame them?

'Help!'
'What just happened?'
'Who are you?'
'Where am I?'
'I can't find my husband!'
They appeared before her, no longer just disembodied voices, and

looking like something from The Walking Dead. They encircled her. Jo felt claustrophobic. Everyone was talking at once. She couldn't make any sense of the gabble. More joined the melee. Dear God, how many were dead? Too many for Jo, in her shocked state, to count. Hands stretched out for her. Voices pleaded with her. They were fading in and out, flickering like the early black and white movies.

Turning on her heel, Jo pushed through them, rushing back outside. Leaning against a wall she took deep breaths and tried to stop her hands shaking. She wished she smoked to calm her nerves, but there was enough smoke clogging the atmosphere without her adding to it.

She hailed the fire commander as he walked past. 'How many dead?'

'Two that we know of. There'll probably be more. It's carnage in there.'

Jo nodded her agreement. Didn't she know it. Carnage and chaos. She felt helpless in the face of it. Her psychic powers were still in their infancy. Still in development. Needing more practice. She clearly needed to take a firm hand. Somehow, she had to talk to one of the dead at a time

As she looked back through the missing window, she saw someone that she hadn't seen before. A new victim? The woman had her back to Jo. Her hair was burned away, leaving a bald fizzing mess. Where the hair and skin on her head had been, it was now burned and split. Her back was red raw, as were the backs of her arms, all her clothes either burnt off or melted into her flesh. As if feeling Jo's scrutiny, the dead woman turned.

Jo's mobile rang. She answered the call, never taking her eyes off the dead woman in front of her.

'Yes?'

'Jo, um,' Byrd said. 'I don't know how to say this. Um...'

So Jo said it for him.

'Judith's dead.'

7

Jo had worked through most of the night with forensics and the emergency services. But now, sat in her office at Chichester Police Station, she was drowning in a sea of tiredness and it was becoming increasingly difficult to keep her eyes open. The smell from her clothes and hair was filling her office with its noxious brew of smoke, fire and blood, not to mention charred flesh. She was going to throw away every stitch of clothing that she was wearing. The vision of the dead and dying was seared into her closed eyelids and she snapped them open, to see the far more endearing sight of Eddie Byrd.

'Boss, you look awful. What are you still doing here? It's five in the morning!'

'To be honest, Eddie, I've no idea. Can't seem to move. I'm trapped in a fog of inertia.'

'Well, snap out of it. You're going home,' and he reached across her desk to use the phone.

Jo was too tired to even berate him for his harsh words. She knew he was right, but she'd wanted to stay at the station until he came in. Just a quick look to make sure he really was alright. Then she could rest. But she wasn't about to tell him that.

Byrd returned the handset to the internal phone on Jo's

desk. 'There's a car standing by to take you home. Come on, let's be having you.'

Glad of a legitimate excuse to have Byrd hold her, Jo leaned on him as they made their way downstairs.

Stopping halfway, she said, 'Eddie, are you really alright?'

'Never better,' he grinned.

'Seriously?'

'Seriously. I'm still a bit shell shocked, but I've been checked over and took something Gill gave me at the hospital to help me sleep for a few hours and I feel much better for it. So now it's your turn. Get a few hours in and come back later this morning, eh?'

Jo nodded and they continued their slow way down the stairs.

'I hear the provisional report is that the seat of the blast was towards the back of the restaurant.'

Jo nodded. 'It looks like a bomb in a briefcase, triggered by mobile phone.'

'We'll work on compiling a list of those killed.'

Jo agreed. 'There's to be an appeal asking for people who suspect a loved one could have been at the restaurant last night to contact us, if they haven't already done so.'

They also needed to replace Judith, urgently. But Jo couldn't face that yet. Another task to add to her already long list of things to do. For once the victims and those missing had been identified, it would be a big job to interview all of their relatives and friends to try and find out who was the target for the bomb and why.

'Who's in charge now?' Eddie asked.

'The Assistant Chief Constable has overall responsibility. We're to report directly to DCI Crooks. This is a big one, Byrd. There'll be large numbers of officers involved, so we'll have to concentrate on whatever part of the investigation Crooks gives us.'

'Understood, Boss.' Eddie let her go and opened the door to the foyer of the police station. As she walked past him, he whispered into her hair, 'Sleep well and I'll be here when you get back.'

She squeezed his hand, then let it go as a uniformed officer approached them. 'The car's ready outside, Ma'am.' Jo thanked him and walked to the car on increasingly wobbly legs. Putting her hand in her pocket, she felt a small tub that wasn't there before. Her fingers closed over it and once in the car she pulled it out. The label on it said the contents were sleeping tablets. Byrd must have slipped it into her pocket. The thoughtful gesture made her smile as she leaned back against the car seat. But to be honest she didn't think she'd have much trouble sleeping, after she'd had a very hot shower that was.

8

As the police car dropped Jo off, the front door flew open and there was her father, still dressed in the clothes he had been wearing when she'd left last night. Feeling like a little girl, Jo crunched through the gravel drive into his arms and promptly cried on his shoulder. Mick held her close until her sobs subsided, then steering her away from the main house, helped her up to her flat above the garage block. She still hadn't spoken, and he didn't press her.

'Go, take those filthy clothes off,' he said and handed her a black sack, pushing her gently towards the bedroom. A few minutes later she emerged wrapped in a dressing gown, to find a cup of herbal tea waiting for her. She swapped it for the black sack, which Mick promptly put outside the front door. She'd only been wearing casual clothes, leggings and a blouse, but the top had been one of her favourites. She couldn't bear to see it again, nor any of her clothes, including her flat black shoes and black coat. Each item would be a reminder of that awful night, if she could ever get the stench of death out of them. No, the rubbish bin was the best place for them.

'I need a shower, or bath,' Jo said. 'I can smell myself.' She gave Mick a stuttering smile.

'Was it bad?'

'Worse than bad. I could see them, Dad. Not just the bodies, but their spirits. Milling around, clothes tattered and torn, bits of them missing, ghosts of the people they used to be. They didn't understand what had happened to them and to be honest, Dad, neither did I.'

'Could you hear them?'

Jo nodded.

'Worse than the Anubis case?'

'Much. It was like an old radio tuning in. Someone would be there and then the next second gone. There was static. Buzzing. Whistling. I've never experienced anything like it. It was horrendous.'

'It might be worth seeing Keith at some point. You know, to get some perspective on it. This is all so sudden and shocking for you, as well as for those who've died.'

Jo nodded. She thought that was a good idea. Keith Thomas had helped her a lot when she'd realised she had a new gift after her riding accident. Mind you, Jo still wasn't sure it was a gift. A member of the local spiritualist church, he'd tried to guide her and educate her about her newfound skills.

Mick reached out and stroked her hair, which was even more of a short, dark, frizzy mess than usual. She used to have long, shoulder-length hair, until Anubis had hacked at it and given her a fringe. One of the first things she'd done after being rescued, was to have a short, pixie haircut, snipping away any trace of the maniac. Somewhere along the way she'd lost the baseball cap she'd been wearing when she left the house. 'Into the shower and then a few hours of sleep for you.'

Jo nodded, then whispered, 'Thanks, Dad,' as he moved towards the door and let himself out of her flat. He'd return to the main house, the heart of the family home. It was where her brothers and their families would visit, without disturbing Jo. The flat above the garages was where she could live her life as she wished. Joining them when she could, or wanted to, and being left alone when she didn't.

She loved her family dearly, but was obsessive about her work, which was by necessity a solitary occupation. One family given up for another. A completely different type of family; a work family that she spent the majority of her time with.

Later, lying in bed, Jo tried to work out why she was seeing the dead. Why the ghostly apparitions were appearing and calling to her? She wasn't touching them, which was how she normally communicated with them. She'd not been able to interact with any of them, just watch them. Perhaps it was the shock. The shock of the dead, not knowing what had happened to them, or why they'd died so suddenly. Jo's shock at what she'd seen, as she'd watched those in the restaurant die.

As she closed her eyes, she couldn't get the image of Judith out of her mind. They'd stood, looking at each other and Jo watched as tears tracked slowly down Judith's face, before she vanished. She needed to go to the morgue later that day, find Judith, and see what she had to tell her. It would be the hardest thing she'd ever done, but a necessary one.

9

It was later that morning when her dad dropped Jo off at the station. She looked up at the building, it's unwelcoming, austere façade, intimidating. Harking back to the 1970's it didn't inspire modern, interconnected police work and all who crossed it's threshold were hoping it would be bulldozed and a modern building take its place.

She pushed open the door and greeted the Desk Sergeant. 'Hi, Jed, how's things?'

'Pretty much as you'd imagine,' he said, looking as exhausted as she felt. 'A bloody bad business this.'

'How long have you been on duty?' she asked.

'Just finishing a double shift, but don't worry, I'll be off soon. Anyway, my troubles are a lot smaller than the poor buggers who lost their lives last night.'

'Amen to that,' agreed Jo.

'Here's some messages for you and Crooks wants you in his office as soon as you arrive. Do not pass go, do not collect £200, just go straight to jail.'

His attempted humour was met with a watery smile and Jo punched the keypad to gain access to the inner workings of the police station. As she tramped up the stairs, she hoped Crooks wouldn't start on her for some perceived misdemeanour. The way she was feeling, she might just give him a mouthful in reply, which wouldn't go down well, nor do her career any good.

'Ah, Jo,' he called as she appeared at his door, coat over one arm and large tote bag in the other. 'Come in. Take a seat.'

'I'll stand thanks, I need to get to my team.'

'Of course, of course. I,' he cleared his throat, 'I just wanted to thank you personally for all your hard work last night. The emergency services are saying that you were single-handedly responsible for finding most of the dead.'

'I doubt, that, Sir,' Jo said. 'I didn't do any more or less than anyone else that was there.' She was well aware that Crooks had stayed away from the disaster site, but thought she'd better not comment on that. She turned to go.

'But, apparently, you seemed to instinctively know where the bodies were.'

His voice stopped her, and she turned back to him, hoping her face was inscrutable.

'How did you manage that?' he probed. 'People are saying it was like you were divining for water.'

Divining for the dead, Jo thought.

'If I didn't know better, I'd think you had some wacky gift.'

'I worked as hard as anyone else down there,' Jo said, 'and the last thing I want is to be singled out for any praise or otherwise. So, if you'll excuse me, Sir?'

Jo didn't wait for an answer and turned on her heel. Clattering down the stairs towards the Major Crimes team offices, she hoped that her dismissal of Crook's comments would put an end to such speculation. The last thing she needed was to be under the scrutiny of the brass. She much preferred to be left alone to work the case in her own way. No one could know of her gift. No one.

10

Jo entered the Major Crimes office, her anxiety evaporating as she was once more in her second home. The familiar wrapped itself around her like a snuggly blanket. She didn't realise how uptight she'd been until then. And so, as the tension left her body, it was replaced by a steely determination. Whoever the bastards were, Jo was determined to find them. Dumping her bag and coat in her office, she then faced what was left of her team.

'OK, what have we got?'

'Hi, Boss,' said DS Byrd, 'good to see you.'

Jo smiled, 'And you and DC Sandy too. How are you, Jill?'

'I'll be alright, Boss. I've only just come in myself. DS Byrd here made me go home last night once I was released from hospital.'

'Any injuries?'

'No, I was lucky.' Jill's green eyes filled with tears. Her fresh-faced, freckled good looks and blond hair verging on ginger usually made her appear far younger than she was. But not today. The loss of Judith and the carnage of the bomb had aged Jo's young DC.

Jo was well aware who Sandy was thinking of. Judith's desk was empty. It was just as she'd left it yesterday. Jo could almost see her still sat at her computer, her muddy coloured straight hair pushed behind her ears, but she had to shake away the tantalising image and concentrate on what DS Byrd was saying.

'Right, Boss, the provisional report from the fire brigade is that the seat of the blast was towards the back of the restaurant. It looks like the bomb was in a briefcase under a table, triggered by mobile phone.'

Jo said, 'Do we know who it was aimed at, or why?'

'All we have at the moment is a list of those killed that we know of so far.'

'Anything interesting stand out?'

'No, Boss. A number of them were staff in the kitchen. It seems the blast took out the wall between the restaurant and the kitchen and then ignited the gas, turning it into a fireball.'

Byrd handed Jo the list of dead and she was studying it when the phone rang on Judith's desk. The three of them looked at it in horror, no one wanting to answer it.

In the end Byrd said, 'Fuck it,' and picked up the receiver. After listening, he then replaced it and said, 'Sandy, turn on the tv.'

The tv was already tuned to the BBC news channel and as they watched the presenter said, 'We now have some breaking news about the incident in Chichester, when a bomb was detonated in an Italian restaurant last night. A national newspaper has received a message from the British Nordic League claiming responsibility. Here's our regional correspondent from the scene in Chichester.

The camera cut away to a young woman, surrounded by empty shops, with a myriad of emergency staff still working away behind her, although it was now a recovery mission, rather than a rescue one. She read from a tablet, with the words appearing on the screen at the same time.

'The British Nordic League wants to rid the UK of the corrupt and incompetent MPs that are supposed to rule our fair country. We need to get rid of them, so better men can take their place and we can live again in peace in a new world. Our motto is to cut out the bad and enrich the good. All the political parties are as bad as each other. We don't discriminate. Any party is fair game. Any corrupt officials better watch their back. I am coming. We are coming. Watch out.'

The young woman's hands shook as she finished, 'The statement is signed by Odin, leader of the British Nordic League.'

Jo turned down the volume.

'Who on earth are the British Nordic League?' asked Jill.

'A UK fascist group who surfaced sometime last year,' said Byrd.

'Fascist group?'

'Yes, Sandy,' said Jo.

'Like in the 1930's and 40's, the black shirts?'

'That's the one,' said Byrd. 'Fascism is named after the fasces, which is an old Roman name for a group of sticks tied together.'

'Sticks? What are you talking about, Byrd?'

'If you'll stop interrupting, and listen,' he smiled at Jo, 'then you'll find out. So, it is easy to break one stick in half.' Byrd demonstrated with his hands, breaking an imaginary stick in two. 'But it is very hard to break many sticks tied together, in half.' This time he mimed being unable to break the sticks no matter how hard he tried. 'Fascists think that everyone rigidly following the same leader and nationalist ideas and ideals, makes the country strong in the same way that the sticks are strong.'

'And Odin?' said Jo.

'An apt name, as he is clearly not opposed to pillage and plunder!'

11

Once the TV had been turned off, Jo said, 'This is going to be much bigger than the Chichester police, or indeed the West Sussex division, can handle,' said Jo. 'So until we're thrown off the case, let's see what we can find out. If Odin is going after corrupt MPs then we better check ours.' Jo had no idea who that was, not having much to do with politics apart from voting. 'Who is our local MP? Find out, then find him, or her.'

The ringing of Jo's mobile interrupted her, and she walked into her office to answer it. Grabbing it off her desk she said, 'Jo Wolfe.'

'Jo, have you just seen the news?'

'Yes, Sir,' Jo answered Alex Crooks' question. 'I'm guessing this means involvement from the police National Counter Terrorism Security Office.'

'Yes and probably MI5. What are you working on at the moment?'

'In the light of that statement we're just trying to trace our MP, Sir.'

'Right oh, keep me posted.'

'Will do, Guv.'

Jo clicked off and returned to Byrd and Sandy. 'Well?'

Jill Sandy said, 'Our MP is Sebastian Truelove.'

'Have you contacted him?'

'Tried to, Boss. Mobile appears to be switched off and he's not answering the phone at home. Neither is his wife…' Jill checked her notes, 'Miranda.'

'Neither of them are replying to texts,' added Byrd.

'Oh, God, he could be one of our victims. And if that press statement is to be believed he was the target and everyone else collateral damage.' Jo closed her eyes. But all that did was to show her the image of Judith as she'd appeared to Jo last night. Snapping them open again, she ordered, 'Get hold of his constituency office or secretary or whoever and find out where he was last night.'

As DC Sandy reached for the phone, Byrd followed Jo into her office. 'You OK, Boss? Only you went a bit pale on me there.'

Jo couldn't tell him the reason, that she'd had a second look at the vision of Judith, so she just smiled and said, 'I'm fine. Just a bit tired.'

Byrd looked as though he was going to say something else but was interrupted by Jill Sandy bursting through the door.

'Guv, his agent says Mr Truelove and his wife should have been at the Italian restaurant last night. They had a table booked for 8pm. He doesn't know for sure that they were there, but he can't raise Mr Truelove either.'

'Come on, Eddie,' Jo said, grabbing her coat. 'Jill, hold the fort.'

'But where are you going, Guv?'

'To the MP's house, of course. Text me his address.'

Sebastian Truelove lived on the outskirts of Chichester and Eddie carved through the traffic in his non-descript dark grey saloon car, with the help of his siren and the flashing lights which were hidden behind the bonnet grill. Within 10 minutes they were there, and he pulled up on the large, empty drive, facing a detached chalet bungalow. The mature property looked well maintained with landscaped front gardens. It was also quiet. Eerily quiet. They sat for a moment, with only the ticking of the cooling engine breaking the silence.

'What's that on the front door?' Eddie asked.

Jo followed his finger. The white door was daubed with red. 'Paint? Done by vandals?'

'Let's have a look.'

They climbed out of the car and walked a few steps to the door.

'It's not paint,' said Eddie squatting down to look closely. 'Jesus Christ. It looks like blood!'

12

Harold Smith was glued to the BBC news channel on the TV in his kitchen. He would normally have been in the Council Chamber by now, but any sessions had been cancelled due to the incident in the city centre. His hand trembled as he ate his cereal, which was rapidly turning to sawdust in his mouth. He looked down at his old-fashioned, striped pyjamas and thought it was about time he got dressed. He noticed a mark on the jacket and picked at it, envisaging it to be dried on muesli. Instead it turned out to be a hole. He sighed. Yet something else that needed replacing.

Being Head of the Planning Committee had been his dream job. He was first to know about proposed developments, what areas had been sanctioned for future development and even the odd building plot, which Smith had been able to buy before it went on the market. Yes, all in all, he loved his job.

It also paid fairly well. But not well enough. Not when you had a demanding wife who spent every waking hour planning shopping trips. And not when you had a propensity for gambling. Not that he was addicted or anything like that. Oh no. But then again, he had just been pouring over the racing pages in his daily newspaper.

He was hoping for a big pay day today, courtesy of his two friends Truelove and Jenkins. They'd each done their bit to make sure the planning consent had gone through smoothly for a huge out of town commercial development. At least the fire being reported on the tv was in the city centre and not on their building plot.

His mobile interrupted his musings. 'Smith,' he snapped.

'Harold, it's John Jenkins. Have you seen the news?'

'Yes, just watching it now.' John Jenkins was Harold's partner in crime. Harold was on the Chichester Council and John on the County Council.

'It seems we could have a problem,' said Jenkins.

'Why? Everything went through smoothly and Truelove was going to collect our payment last night. Where was the meet?' asked Harold.

'There wasn't a meet. A case was being left for him to collect.'

'Left where? Oh shit. Oh God! Tell me it's not true!'

'Sorry, but it is true. Trulove was collecting the money from that Italian restaurant that blew up.'

'What the fuck! I don't believe this! No Truelove. No money and lots of police involvement.' Harold's shaking hand was now decidedly wobbly. He was having trouble holding his mobile without bashing himself on his ear.

'Precisely,' said Jenkins. 'You'd better get your ducks in a row and delete any incriminating evidence pronto.'

'Yes, yes, of course.'

'And don't contact me ever again,' said Jenkins and cut the call.

Harold took a few moments. He looked at his cereal bowl. Then at his mobile. And finally at the TV, which was still showing pictures of Chichester city centre. He sighed and stood up. He'd better go and get dressed and get on with it.

'Oh, there you are, Harold,' said his wife when he trudged into the bedroom. 'Have you seen this?' and she pointed to the wardrobe door which was hanging drunkenly on one hinge. 'The bloody thing just broke in my hand!'

'Oh dear,' he said.

'Oh dear? Bugger oh dear, you'd better fix it,' and she stormed out of the bedroom.

'Where are you going?' he shouted after her.

'Shopping. On my own,' and the front door slammed behind her.

Harold shook his head and sat down heavily on the bed. It was definitely going to be a particularly shitty day.

13

'Right,' said Jo. 'We're going to have to treat this as a crime scene.' She pulled her mobile out of her pocket and called Bill.

As he answered she could hear the weariness in his voice. She quickly told him where she was and why and that she needed forensic support.

'I've only got one person free at the moment and that's me. Mind you I've got to attend a divisional meeting about the restaurant blast. So I've only an hour.'

'That's fine. Thanks, Bill. We'll talk to the neighbours while we're waiting for you.' She returned her mobile to her pocket.

'Left, or right?' said Byrd who'd heard the conversation.

'Both,' said Jo. 'Let's start with the right.'

'Your right, or my right?' He was stood opposite her, not next to her.

'Shut up, Byrd,' Jo said, smiling. 'I'm the boss, so my right.'

They crunched down the gravel drive to the road and rounded the corner to an equally desirable residence.

'Bloody hell,' said Byrd. 'People around here have money.'

'Don't they just,' agreed Jo.

All the properties were large, detached, well maintained and set back from the traffic on the main road into Chichester. The neighbouring property to Truelove's house was mock-Georgian, complete with white columns and symmetrical windows. The door was answered by an attractive, blond haired, forty something woman in exercise gear. She clearly wasn't expecting a call from the police.

'Oh, sorry, I was just on my way out…' the sentence hung in the air, the woman clearly having no intention of inviting them in.

'And you are?' Byrd asked.

'Jan Starling. Perhaps you've heard of my husband?' There was that pause again.

'No,' Jo said, becoming irritated by the airhead in front of her. 'Should we?' Without giving the woman time to answer, Jo continued, 'We're here about your neighbours, the Truelove's?'

'Oh, Sebastian and Miranda?'

'Yes. Do you know them well?'

'Sure, Miranda goes to the same gym as me. In fact,' she glanced at her watch, 'she's late. I thought it was her calling, we go to Pilates today.'

'When did you last see them?'

'I caught a glimpse of them last night as they left for dinner. They were going to that Italian in town everyone's raving about these days.'

'Have you seen them since?'

'What? Um, no I don't believe I have.' Then the penny finally dropped. 'Oh my God. The Italian! You don't think? I mean… were they?'

'We don't know, we're trying to trace them.'

'Aren't they in?' she peered over their heads looking at the drive next door.

'We can't get an answer.'

'I, I've got a key. Would that help?'

Jo smiled, 'Yes, it would, thanks.'

Jan took a step backwards and reached to her left. There

was the sound of a door being opened and then the rattle of keys. 'Here,' she pressed a set of keys into Byrd's outstretched hand. 'Shall I?' she took a step forward.

'No,' said Jo. 'Thank you but there's no need for you to accompany us. DS Byrd will let you know what's happening.'

'Oh, right, yes. Thank you,' she backed away, leaving the door open and sat down on the stairs, all poise gone in an instant, leaving an emotional woman, wondering what had happened to her friends.

'Another indication that they were at the restaurant last night,' said Byrd as they walked back to the Truelove's house.

'I know,' nodded Jo. 'It's not looking good.'

They turned at the sound of a vehicle behind them. For a moment Jo hoped it was the Truelove's car, but it was only Bill pulling into the drive. Jo and Byrd approached the car, asking Bill to take samples of the paint or blood, or whatever it was, off the door and then to wait while they searched the premises.

Pulling on gloves they then entered the hall, calling out that they were from Chichester Police.

There was no reply.

Once again there was that eerie quiet and all the noise from outside was shut out once the front door was closed behind them. Jo called out again, but there was still no response.

They made their way through to a bright, spacious lounge which looked like a Barker and Stonehouse display, all high-end furniture, with nothing out of place, but with no personality.

It was the kitchen that drew a whistle from Byrd. The high gloss white units and black marble work surfaces, with an impressive island, led through to an open dining space. Bifold doors gave access to the gardens, which were clearly looked after by an experienced gardener.

'How the hell do you afford this on an MPs salary?' he

asked.

'You don't. You either have family money. Or an alternative income stream.'

'I'm betting on the latter,' he said, and Jo nodded her agreement.

They quickly checked the remaining rooms which turned out to be bedrooms and two bathrooms before walking outside.

'There's no one there,' Jo said talking to Bill. 'If they were at the restaurant last night, then how come their bodies haven't been found?'

Bill scratched his bald head. 'My guess is that it's because they were closest to the blast. If it was under their table, say, they'd be pretty much incinerated. All that might be left is the odd body part, so I'll take something for DNA comparison, but I have to say it looks like they were there, don't you think?'

'I'll go back in and get something for you,' Jo said.

'Do you want me to go, Boss?'

'No, that's OK, I won't be a minute.'

Jo went in the house and ran up the stairs. In the master en-suite bathroom she collected two toothbrushes from the mug on the sink. Opening a side cupboard, she found a hairbrush with long, blond hair caught in it. Mrs Truelove's.

As Jo grabbed it, the bathroom faded, and she had a sensation of falling. Then a huge flash, that reminded Jo of a photographer's flash bulb, made Jo stumble backwards against the bath.

And then there she was. Miranda Truelove. Her hair was a wild halo around her head. Her face blackened with soot. Naked; her clothes presumably lost in the explosion. Her skin was ripped away, leaving raw, red, weeping flesh. She looked angry. Jo wasn't sure if it was aimed at her, for disturbing the dead. But her words seemed to imply not.

'It's all his fault, the greedy bastard. He never had enough. Always wanting more, more, more...' and as Miranda pulled at her face, globs of flesh came away in her hands.

Her words were more inside Jo, rather than spoken out loud. They

34

reverberated around her head. Insistent. Demanding to be heard. Then Miranda Trulove, or what was left of her, emitted a cry of such pain and sorrow that it couldn't be ignored. She reached into her lower stomach and grabbed another handful of gore, holding it out to Jo. This time instead of red blubber, there was a small form. A foetus. Miranda Truelove had been pregnant.

Mercifully, she then faded away. Jo was shaken, both by the sighting and by the message it contained. She had gone cold from head to foot, her teeth were chattering and goose bumps appeared on her arms. It felt as if Miranda had passed through Jo on her way to goodness knows where. Jo rubbed her arms to generate some warmth, then stopped. She had the eery feeling that her own flesh would peel away, just like Miranda Truelove's had done. She had to get out of the house.

Collecting her samples and pushing them into evidence bags with shaking fingers, Jo fled. But even as she ran, she wondered what Miranda Truelove had been talking about. What the hell had their MP been mixed up in?

14

Welcome to the website of the British Nordic League.
Making Britain a better place for the British.

I'm sure your first question will be: What do the British Nordic
League stand for?
To answer that, consider the following edict from Norse
mythology.

-Völuspá
In the poem, a völva (a female seer) recites information to Odin.
In stanza 41, the völva says:
"It sates itself on the lifeblood of fated men,
paints red the powers' homes with crimson gore.
Black become the sun's beams in the summers that follow,
weathers all treacherous. Do you still seek to know? "

Stanzas from Völuspa were performed in song form by the
Vikings and used as battle chants. Prophecy of the Völva is the first
and best-known poem of the Poetic Edda. It tells the story of the
creation of the world and its coming end, related to the audience by a
völva addressing Odin.

This is one of the most important primary sources for the study of

Norse mythology. Henry Adam Bellows proposed that it was written in the 10th-century and written by a pagan Icelander with knowledge of Christianity. He also assumed the early listeners would have been very familiar with the "story" of the poem.

The prophecy is that all the Gods will be killed and finally a beautiful reborn world will rise from the ashes of death and destruction.

So, the British Nordic League will seek out corrupt politicians who will be killed and we will 'paint red the powers' homes with crimson gore'. We will rid the country of them, so better men can take their place and we can live again in a new world.
Are you with us?
ODIN

Upon her return to the police station, Jo sought out Crooks.

'What do you want us to do, Boss?' she asked. 'We have 12 victims so far and two we are pretty sure are our local MP and his wife. Coupled with the warning from Odin, it looks like he was the target and the others were very unfortunate collateral damage, which very nearly included all of my team. I want these bastards.'

Crooks said, 'Work the MP angle and let the other agencies try and find the organisation.'

'Who's the police officer acting as liaison? Is it the ACC?'

'No, it's me.' He looked closely at her. 'Do you have a problem with that?'

Jo took a step back, 'Of course not, Sir. It means we'll be in closer contact than normal, of course.'

'Exactly, so I look forward to working with you again, DI Wolfe.'

Jo fled his office, mumbling something about having pressing interviews.

Fuck.

In the cool of the stairwell she stopped and placed her

flaming cheek against the frigid wall. It shouldn't worry her that much, working with her boss. It was just that Alex Crooks was the person she nearly had an affair with. Since then they'd kept each other at arm's length. Jo was autonomous, running her group of officers. It clearly was to be different on this case. They'd need to know that each other had the latest information on the case. Information that could benefit them both.

Their past friendship, for that's all it was at least on her side, couldn't be allowed to impact her relationship with Byrd. She fervently hoped that Crooks wouldn't bugger that up for her. He could do, even though nothing sexual happened between Jo and Crooks. If he found out about Byrd, he could wreak his revenge on Jo by destroying her relationship with her sergeant.

The thing was, Crooks hadn't been able to persuade his wife that his friendship with Jo was anything more than a close working relationship. Mrs Crooks was a jealous woman by nature and nothing Alex said or did could persuade her that she had nothing to be jealous about. Adding to the mix her husband's total dedication to the job, the toxic brew meant she had walked out on him.

Anyway there was nothing to be done, so Jo just had to knuckle down and get on with it and try to find a safe path through the mine field of jealousy and anger.

15

Unable to put it off any longer, Jo went to see Judith at the mortuary. She'd had the nod earlier in the day from Jeremy that her post-mortem had been done and Jo could see her if she wanted to. Jo wanted to. Very much.

The morgue at St Richards was deadly quiet. After the hurly burly of the day, as the team had fought to keep up with the bodies arriving seemingly without end, everyone had gone home for a well-deserved rest. They wouldn't be back until 6am the following morning.

Jo stole across to the chill containers that held the bodies. On the front of each drawer was the name and file number of the deceased. Judith was slap bang in the middle. As Jo held out her hand to pull open the drawer, it trembled. She hadn't seen Judith in the flesh since the restaurant, only in spirit form, so she wasn't sure what to expect.

As it happened there was very little damage to the front of Judith. All the damage was on her back. The back of her head, her back, the backs of her arms and legs. Jo lifted the protective linen sheet as far as she needed, to show her Judith's face.

Jo gulped back the lump in her throat as she looked at her friend and colleague. Gone for good. Never coming back. It was almost the undoing of her. Through her tears she felt for Judith's hand and grabbed hold.

Instead of the blast at the restaurant, Jo saw a selection of snapshot moments. Judith at work and at home with her family. In all of them Judith was happy, smiling and content with her life. Jo was reminded of good times. The summer BBQ they'd had that turned into a wash out. The trip to the cinema to see what turned out to be a bloody awful film. A rare shopping trip for Jo, as Judith helped her choose a new trouser suit, being unable to persuade Jo to buy a dress. Judith marrying her husband and having two beautiful girls. That was the overall feeling Jo got from touching Judith. It was a fitting way for them to say goodbye to each other.

Letting go of Judith's hand, Jo was sure she'd see her friend again. There was still one last job for them to do together. To get Odin. Jo knew she'd need all the help from the dead that she could muster. She could sense that he was going to be a formidable opponent and one that certainly wouldn't go down without a fight.

16

By the next morning they had confirmation that DNA found at the scene matched that of the Trueloves' DNA taken from their house.

'OK, so this part of the investigation is ours,' Jo told Byrd and Sandy. 'The first thing we need is access to his computer, laptop, tablet, phones, all of it. Both work and personal. Diary, the lot. If you can't find itemised mobile phone bills, get them from the provider. We'll comb through them and highlight any shall we say odd communications, or ones that fall into a pattern.'

'Um, Guv,' said Byrd interrupting her. 'Jill and I can't do this on our own. We need help.'

'I know,' Jo sighed. 'That's why we have a new girl coming in.' Jo grabbed a file from her desk. 'Sasha Gold.'

'I know her,' said Jill.

'Really?'

'Yeah, she joined the force at the same time as me.'

'Oh, good, that'll help her fit in. A friendly face and all that.'

'Yes, but…'

'But?'

'Um, well, we took different career paths. It's just that Sasha isn't normal police material. She has awesome computer skills but is rather lacking in personal ones, if you see what I mean.'

'Well, not to worry. All I care about at the moment is the awesome computer skills,' said Jo, hoping to put a lid on any dissent. There'd be enough rumours swirling around once Sasha was in-situ and people began to ask who the new girl was. According to Sasha's personnel file she was being sent over from another investigative group, who couldn't wait to get rid of her. Maybe it was a female/male thing? Whatever it was they just didn't get her at all. Jo hoped she could do better than the blokes on that one and help Sasha fit in.

But she had to admit that it was so strange looking over and not seeing Judith at her desk. Jo was battling with her sadness over the death of her friend and colleague. The other thing was the fact that Judith kept appearing, showing herself to Jo. But could Judith really help with the investigation? There'd been no words spoken between them, rather Jo having the feeling of Judith simply urging her on.

Don't forget me. Find out what happened. Avenge my death.

Jo felt a prickle at the back of her neck, a soft breath, and then it was gone. Judith.

Yet Jo had a vague feeling of unease. She wasn't sure if she could trust her instincts. Was it Jo's sadness and need that was making Judith appear? Was it that Jo couldn't let Judith go, rather than the other way around?

Jo felt on the back foot, being drawn along by the investigation, rather than leading it. But she guessed that was because it was such a large operation. She was only a tiny cog in the wheel, not the biggest fish in the sea. She smiled at her mix of idioms. That just about summed her up; a mixed-up mess of emotions.

But she couldn't get the questions out of her head. Was Jo being misled? Was it really Judith she was seeing and feeling? Or some other spirt manifesting itself in the guise of Judith, exploiting Jo's vulnerability and weakness?

Her introspection was getting her nowhere and so it was

with some relief that she spied someone walking towards her, determination in every stride, clutching a large cardboard box. Sasha.

'Is this me?' she asked and dumped her box without waiting for a reply. Jo could see the look of horror on the faces of Byrd and Sandy as Sasha put the box on Judith's desk. Then they both attempted to fix their faces into more normal looking features. Jo was glad of that. It wasn't Sasha's fault their friend and colleague had died in the worst possible way.

'If you're Sasha Gold, then yes, that's your desk. I'm DI Jo Wolfe.' Jo held out her hand for Sasha to shake but it was ignored. In fact the girl wasn't even looking at Jo. Nonplussed, she continued, 'That's DS Eddie Byrd and DC Jill Sandy.'

Sasha eventually looked up, under her lashes, quickly nodded in their direction and then turned her attention back to the box. Jo was beginning to see what Jill meant already. Oh well, at least Sasha didn't seem to be trying to take Judith's place by holding out the hand of friendship. And after all, as long as she was good at her job, what did it matter? She guessed they'd get used to Sasha's ways eventually.

17

By the following morning they had a thread of a lead. Eddie explained the steps they'd taken so far. 'It looks like our MP Sebastian Truelove was having an affair.'

'Despite the attractive wife? She was a model, wasn't she?'

'Yes, she was. I found that strange as well,' said Jill. 'Why would you play away when you have a trophy wife at home?'

'Maybe she has too many headaches,' Eddie laughed.

Ignoring him, Jo asked how long it had been going on.

'Looks like about three months. What do you want us to do, Boss?'

Jo considered for a moment, then said, 'Do a complete background check on her. I think we need to see if she was a genuine partner, or if it was someone with a completely different agenda that included harming our dearly beloved member of parliament.' Jo wasn't sure if the woman would have any bearing on the investigation, but it paid to be thorough.

Jill said, 'There are receipts for a local hotel on the dates that tally with the mobile phone calls.'

'Good, go and interview the reception staff. They can be a mine of information. They see everything and say nothing.'

'Yes, Boss.'

Jill returned to her desk and sat down, hands on her keyboard.

'Now, DC Sandy,' Jo said exasperated. 'Byrd go with her.'

'Boss,' Sasha called without looking at Jo, having just taken a phone call. 'DCI Crooks wants to see you. He said,' Sasha looked at her pad, 'to tell her to get a bloody move on, I've haven't got all day.'

'OK,' said Jo, wondering why Sasha had repeated the message word for word. Shaking her head, she did as she was asked.

Once in Crooks' office it transpired there was an inter-agency meeting he wanted her to attend with him, so she spent the next two hours listening to dry presentations on where they were up to with the investigation. None of which moved things forward that Jo could see, or at least that appertained to her part of the case. She was glad she could report the seizing of Truelove's devices and that they were pretty sure he was having an affair. Crooks looked pleased, but she wondered why he hadn't told her about the meeting and given her some time to gather her thoughts. Maybe he thought she'd refuse to go with him. Anyway as there was a distinct lack of females around the table, Jo was glad she'd batted one for the girls.

She'd just returned to her office when Byrd and Sandy returned from the Chichester Harbour Hotel, looking rather pleased with themselves.

'Ah, there you are. How did you get on? Rather well by the looks of you.'

'We were right and we were wrong,' said Byrd.

'So he was having an affair?'

'He certainly was.'

'But with a man!' blurted Sandy as though she couldn't keep the news in any longer.

'Oh my God,' said Jo. 'He was gay!'

'Yes, but not many people knew. He'd not come out.'

'It seems he used the Hotel Spa as cover. He's a member there, so he had a legitimate reason for being in the hotel.'

'It's just that sometimes he booked a room as well as a massage.'

'So you think this is the mysterious O from his phone?' Jo asked. 'Who is he?'

'No one seems to know his name. although there are a few more staff to interview who weren't on duty when we went over.'

'Is that why he was corrupted? Not just for the kickbacks he was taking as payment for favours done, but to keep his secret safe, do you think?' said Jo.

'That's possible, but it does appear to have been an open secret, in the hotel at least,' said Byrd.

'Did you manage to get a description of this mysterious partner of his?'

'Just a brief one. Tall, lean, good looking, a mane of blond hair. Some staff reckoned he was too good for Truelove. Certainly the women found him very attractive and said it was a waste that he appeared to be gay!'

'Tall, lean, a mane of blond hair,' murmured Jo. Then she added in a much louder voice, 'O.'

'Sorry?' said Byrd.

'O for Odin. That tallies with the phone calls. The number was saved as 'O'. It looks like Truelove could have been having an affair with our bomber.'

18

'What else has Truelove been up to? That's not enough surely. Not enough to be bombed,' Eddie insisted.

'OK,' said Jo. 'Let's keep that thought going. What are we looking for?'

'God knows, it could be anything.' Byrd ran a hand through his dark hair in exasperation. Longer on top and shorter on the sides, Byrd had a modern haircut. Running his hands through it didn't make a mess as it just flopped back into place. Jo hated him for it. Hair that stayed in place and in shape was an anathema to her. No matter what she did to hers, it fell where it wanted and not where she wanted. Maybe she should try a different hairdresser, or even use Byrd's.

Then Sasha said, 'No it couldn't,' and jolted Jo back to earth, by joining the discussion, although she hadn't been asked to. Jo looked askance. She was still trying to get used to the girl's blunt, brusque manner.

'Sorry?' asked Jill.

'It couldn't be just anything. There's a recognised set of corruption types.'

'There is?'

'Yes.

'And you know what they are?'

'Of course.'

'Put them up on the board please, Sasha,' Jo said and handed the girl a whiteboard pen.

Sasha stood and without looking at any of them moved to the board keeping her back to the team. They watched as she wrote:

Bribery, trading in influence or patronage.

Nepotism and cronyism.

Electoral fraud.

Embezzlement.

Kickbacks.

Unholy alliance.

Then she scurried back to her desk and bent her head, hiding behind her curtain of hair.

'What the hell?' said Byrd.

'What do those even mean, Sasha?' asked Jill.

'Oh very well,' huffed Sasha and she went on to give an explanation of each one, in a tone that said the others were too thick to know these things and showed her exasperation. Jo decided to ignore all of that as Sasha was imparting good information that they needed to hear.

'I would have thought bribery, trading in influence and patronage speak for themselves. It's those who will do what someone wants them to and pays them well for, or those who have secrets they want to keep buried. I think that Truelove certainly traded in influence, accepted payments for exerting his influence in government committees, or local ones and no doubt got paid for being a patron of charities and the like.

'Of course nepotism and cronyism are two favourites. It could even be a Freemason thing. You know, only using those companies or organisations that follow the "you pat my back and I'll pat yours" way of doing business.

'Electoral fraud is a big no no, but it happens. Maybe spending too much on advertising and trying to hide the cost. Hiding big donations by breaking them down into smaller ones and using murky accounting. Of course this could be on a local, national or even international scale.

'And then we have embezzlement. Spending funds that aren't yours. Or putting in the books an inflated salary of an employee and pocketing the different between what you show and what he actually earns, for instance.

'And then there's the old favourite, kickbacks. That wouldn't surprise me, what with Truelove's record. The latest scheme he's been involved with is the new out of town development. I don't know the details yet, but he certainly backed the scheme, saying how good it would be for the local area, bringing with it much needed jobs. Let's face it he had to pay for that designer kitchen somehow.

'I kind of figure that unholy alliance in this instance is similar to the Theodore Roosevelt campaign against the "invisible government, the unholy alliance between corrupt business and corrupt politics." It looks like that is what Odin is fighting. Corruption undermines the legitimacy of government and such democratic values as trust and tolerance. A state of unrestrained political corruption is known as a kleptocracy, literally meaning "rule by thieves".'

'Bloody hell,' said Jill. 'No wonder they call you Wiki.'

'Jill!' admonished Jo.

'Sorry,' her young DC mumbled.

All Sasha said was, 'Mmmm,' shrugged her shoulders and turned to her computer.

'While we think about what Sasha has just told us, perhaps food would be a good idea. Anyone else hungry?'

'Yes,' chorused Jill and Byrd, but Sasha shook her head.

'Fancy pizza?' Byrd asked.

Jo said, 'Bad idea, Eddie. I don't think I can eat Italian food ever again.'

'Why on earth would you say that?' said Sasha, who clearly hadn't made the emotional connection.

Jo looked at her speechless and horrified. Jill Sandy emitted a strangled sob and ran out of the office. Eddie slumped forward and put his head in his hands.

'I'm vegan,' Sasha said, apropos of nothing.

'Of course you are,' said Jo. What else would she expect? It seemed working with Sasha wasn't going to be easy.

19

Stephen McGrath stood in his bedroom, in front of the mirrored wardrobe, wrapped only in a towel. Droplets of water from his shower still clung to his torso. In fact that was where his attention was. On his chest to be precise and on the scar running down his breastbone. It always reminded him of the ancient punishment, "hung, drawn and quartered", although he'd only been drawn. But he felt like a criminal all the same. He turned away, as if turning away from his crime. But, of course, it wasn't that simple.

The morning suit hung from a hook on the back of his bedroom door. It was a great day for the family, the marriage of his only child, Hope. The arrangements had been minutely scrutinised, every possible scenario poured over, until final decisions were made.

The venue, a large Jacobean manor house, was exquisite. The rooms elegant and perfect. The cost, eye-wateringly expensive. But, of course, worth every penny to see the happiness shining from Hope's eyes. His daughter was beautiful of image and heart. She was a kind and generous soul, loved by everyone, worshiped by her husband to be.

But her father? Well that was another matter altogether. He might look distinguished, good for his age and any other plaudit you'd care to add, but inside he was black. Evil. He might have a new heart, but at what price? Beating inside his chest was the heart of an innocent man who'd been in the wrong place at the wrong time. A car crash had taken his life, abruptly and unexpectedly. Stephen had been the lucky recipient of the beating organ. The problem was it had nothing to do with luck, and everything to do with coercion. A few words in the right ears and a large cheque, meant he'd miraculously been pushed to the top of the transplant list, trampling over other deserving souls who had died whilst on the list since Stephen's operation. Just because he had money.

The grief and pain felt by their relatives, caused by his own grubby morals, didn't bear thinking about. Stephen was much happier with his head in the sand, refusing to think about what he'd done. But today of all days brought the reality home to him. If he hadn't had the heart transplant, he wouldn't be alive to see his daughter's marriage.

A head popped through the bedroom door. 'Oh, Stephen, you're not dressed yet! Hope is waiting for you!'

He could hear the panic in his wife's voice. He gave her his best politician's smile. 'I'll only be a few minutes, don't worry, everything will be perfect today. Trust me.'

Her eyes filled with tears and she nodded. He didn't think those would be the only tears his wife would shed today. Tears of happiness. And Stephen's tears? Well those would be tinged with grief for the people he'd killed as he'd clambered over them to reach the top of the transplant list.

20

The British Nordic League
Making Britain a better place for the British.

With European elections taking place, right-wing nationalists and the far right all across Europe are sensing an opportunity. Nationalism has always been a feature across Europe's political spectrum but there has been a recent rise in voter support for right-wing and populist parties.

Italy's nationalist League formed a populist coalition in Italy. Spain - once thought a barren ground for such politics - elected multiple far-right politicians to parliament for the first time since the country returned to democracy in 1975. And until this week, Austria's Freedom Party was in coalition with the centre right.

In part, this can be seen as a backlash against the political establishment, but the wave of discontent also taps into concerns about globalisation, immigration, a dilution of national identity and the EU itself.

We've already shown that corrupt British officials are fair game. There are others in our sights. You have been warned.
ODIN

Byrd and Sandy were going through Truelove's business diaries and correspondence, with Sasha accessing his on-line calendar and emails. Meanwhile, Jo was writing yet another bloody report for Crooks to present at the Divisional Meetings. It seemed to Jo that was all she was doing these days. Normal police investigation seemed to have been suspended for the duration. The great, lumbering behemoth of a case was crashing through the UK, devouring everything in its path, but as far as she could see, not actually doing anything about finding Odin and stopping him. Her frustration boiled over and she had to get out of the claustrophobic office. She was spending far too long indoors.

She grabbed her coat and marched out of her office. 'Byrd, you're with me,' she called. If she was going to escape with someone to keep her company, Eddie was her man. In more ways than one. Which made her smile inside.

Eddie ran to keep up with her and finally stopped her on the steps outside of the police station.

He looked around to check they were alone then said, 'Jo, what's the matter?' He never called her Jo if anyone was within earshot. 'You've just pulled me off an important job. This better be good.'

'Maybe not good, but important.'

'That's it, no further explanation?'

'None. Come on,' and Jo strode off down the road.

She stopped at a coffee shop. 'Two take away coffees please, Byrd.'

He rolled his eyes, but went in. While Jo waited, she put her hands into the pockets of her Paddington duffle coat. She'd loved it the minute she'd clapped eyes on it in the sale in some shop or other. She couldn't remember which one. The whimsical nature of it appealed. At times her job required her to be solemn and staid and as she wore androgynous type suits at work, at least her spirits were lifted by her duffle coat. Mind you, since her relationship with Byrd, she'd found herself more and more wearing sensual silk blouses with her suits. She realised she was no Gillian Anderson but could live in hope. Every woman she knew who'd watched The Fall wanted to look like Gillian.

Byrd strode out of the shop and they took their coffees to the Cathedral grounds and sat facing the winter sun. Jo looked up at the building that to her, at least, looked part cathedral and part castle. The square towers seemed incongruous with the spire towering over them. After almost one thousand years, the Cathedral was still a vital part of the local community - as a place of worship and a place of tourism and heritage. Even as they sat there, there were school groups, Chinese tourists and older couples, all on a day out. Parts of the cathedral were shrouded in scaffolding and plastic, protecting the ongoing restoration work, but it didn't seem to have stopped the tourists.

'There, isn't that better, don't you think? I was so sick of my view of the office walls, I thought I'd swop them for the cathedral walls.'

Byrd grinned, 'Yes, Boss, whatever you say.'

'I just had to get out, Eddie. This whole huge investigation thing is getting me down.'

'How many agencies involved now?'

'Let me see, too bloody many. Gold Commanders, MI5, Terrorism, National Crime Agency, Government minister, Fire Brigade commander, and others that I can't remember who on earth they are. I tell you it's doing my head in, Eddie. I'm used to investigation, being out and about, not stuck behind a bloody desk writing reports that no one reads.'

'You don't know they don't read them.'

'I'm pretty sure they don't. Oh well.'

'So why are we here?'

'This is an update meeting, albeit in a beautiful location and the fresh air. Anything from Truelove's diaries?'

'We've been through his business diary but there's nothing that could be called out of the ordinary. Just stuff from constituents, and daily workings of parliament. Sasha's not been able to find anything on his computer, tablet or phone either.'

'So no smoking gun?'

'No, sorry, Jo.'

'Mmm,' she murmured. 'So how do we find out what he doesn't want found?' She finished her coffee. 'Come on, we're going back to his house.'

'Okay, but first,' and Byrd leaned forward to give her a lingering kiss. 'Only if you agree to see me tonight.'

Jo laughed and batted him away. 'Find me some evidence to pin on Truelove first and then you're on!'

21

'What the hell are you doing? I told you never to contact me again.'

Harold Smith could hear the anger in Jenkins' voice, but it was tinged with fear. And that's why he'd rung. He was bloody frightened too.

'Relax I'm ringing from a phone box.'

'What the hell do you want?'

'I needed to know what was going on. Have you heard from the police at all?'

'No, why have you?'

'No. So it seems we're safe for now.'

'Safe! Well we would be safe if you'd stop ringing me!'

'This is the only time I've rung! Come on, John, that's not fair.'

'Oh alright, sorry. But no I've not had anyone asking me about Truelove, or the incident at the restaurant. So, how are you holding up?'

'Not well. I'm jumping at everything. A doorbell. Car door slamming. Phone ringing. I tell you, John, I can't take much more of this.'

'There's not been anything on the news about a wider investigation, so I'm taking the view that we're pretty safe.'

'I hope you're right,' said Smith. He opened his mouth

to say more, but Jenkins had put the phone down.

He left the phone box, looking left and right in case anyone had been watching him, or following him. But he didn't think they had. He couldn't see anyone acting suspiciously. Only himself. He likened himself to a Mr Bean character, all tweed jacket, knitted tie and bumbling accidents. Knee jerk reactions to things that went wrong. The trouble was he'd really needed his cut of the money in that briefcase. But he was beginning to think there hadn't been any in there at all. A smoking case, rather than a smoking gun.

He went into the corner shop. 'Twenty Players Super Kings red, please,' he asked the assistant on the till.

'I didn't know you smoked, Harold,' she said as she scanned the packet. 'That'll be £9 please.'

'I don't smoke very often,' he replied. 'They're too bloody expensive.' As he spoke, he was digging in his pocket. He found his £10 note, and pulled it out, to find it was only a fiver. Oh God, the embarrassment. 'Gosh, sorry, I thought it was £10!'

'Got your card, love?'

'No, I've forgotten it,' Smith lied, knowing full well he hadn't brought it because there was no money left in the account.

'Not to worry. Here,' she said. 'I'll take the £5 and you can pop the £4 in later. I'll put a note in the till.'

'Oh, right, thanks, thanks a lot.'

Harold had to stop himself running out of the shop before the woman changed her mind. His latest top tip had fallen at the first hurdle and wiped out his meagre bank balance. Maybe he'd find some money in his wife's purse? Mind you, she tended to keep it under lock and key these days. He couldn't blame her. So he'd just have to scour the house for some change. Perhaps there would be some coins down the back of the sofa. At least he'd be able to have a cigarette while he searched.

22

Jo and Byrd pulled up outside Truelove's house. It hadn't taken long before their home had taken on an air of desolation. It was quiet. Empty. Lifeless and soulless. Trails of police tape blew in the breeze, snapping and whistling.

As they stood outside the front door, Jo said, 'There must be something else. We need private stuff, diary, different mobile phone, tablet, anything like that.'

'We've taken everything we saw, Jo.'

'I know, but let's see if we can find anything hidden. Anything incriminating that Truelove wanted to keep out of the public eye.'

'Okay, you're the Boss. You start upstairs, I'll do down here.'

Searches were messy things. Not that Jo and Byrd would be deliberately disrespectful, but when you were searching for something hidden, you inevitably made waves. You'd check under mattresses, inside mattresses, the bottom of furniture in case there's a package taped there, or hidden in air vents, or safes concealed behind pictures. Every nook and cranny had to be inspected.

But she couldn't find anything. Jo went downstairs and met Byrd in the hall.

'Anything?' he asked.

'No. You?'

He shook his head. 'Where to now?'

'His constituency office.'

There wasn't much to search there. Only one office and a large open room at the front where the constituents walked in off the street. Walking around the office Jo moaned, 'Bloody hell, I was sure we'd find something.'

'Mmm,' mumbled Byrd, who was walking over the rug in front of Truelove's desk.

'Byrd, what are you doing? Why are you wearing a path in that carpet?'

'Shhh.' He put up a hand to stop her talking, as if she hadn't got the idea already. 'Can you hear something?' he carried on pacing.

'Yeah, it sounds like a creaking floorboard.' Then Jo did a double take. 'Creaking floorboard?'

'Exactly, here give me a hand.'

They rolled the carpet up together, no mean feat as it covered most of the floor. And then there it was. The source of the creaking. A loose floorboard. Rooting around on Truelove's desk, Jo found a letter opener and passed it to Byrd, who used it to lever up the wood. They both peered down a hidey hole. Byrd plunged his hand in and felt around. The first thing he withdrew was a leather-bound pocket-book, closed with a band. The second was a padded envelope.

Byrd placed both items on a plastic evidence bag Jo had laid on the floor. They'd found Truelove's little black book. Along with details of an offshore account and a key for a deposit box at a local bank. As Jo touched the book, she was immediately rocked back on her heels by a vision.

She saw Truelove and Odin (at least he looked like Odin using the hotel employees' description) at the health spa in the hotel. The two men went into the sauna. Odin sat close to Truelove and whispered in his ear. His breath played against Truelove's ear and then neck. Jo could feel the shivers go down Truelove's back and his body responding to the attention. He couldn't believe that this wonderful, erotic and sensual man could be interested in him. A lowly backbench MP, but one with connections he had to admit. Truelove was completely under Odin's spell. He would do anything for the gorgeous God before him. He had to keep Odin close to him and interested and if the price was using his influence to Odin's advantage, then what harm could it do? And the sums of money being bandied around were not inconsiderable.

Yes, Truelove was happy being influenced and seduced by Odin.

Byrd was over the other side of the room and didn't notice what Jo was doing, which was in essence, nothing. She slipped the book and papers into the evidence bag, then busied herself looking through Truelove's desk, her cheeks flaming. She hoped Byrd didn't suspect anything. Didn't know about her gift. Fancy having a vision right in front of him! She couldn't lose Byrd. Because of what they'd just found he'd be coming over that night with a takeaway and wine. And wouldn't be leaving until the following morning. At least not if Jo had anything to do with it. She'd do anything to keep Byrd. She was completely under his spell. The similarity between her and Truelove wasn't lost on Jo. But of course Jo wasn't doing anything illegal to keep her man. She had morals. Truelove? Not so much.

23

The pain in his chest hit without warning. One minute Stephen McGrath was sleeping peacefully in his bed, the next he was thrust into his worst nightmare. A heart attack. The worst possible scenario for a heart transplant patient. As the pain travelled down his arm he began gasping for breath. He was relieved to see his wife and daughter burst into the bedroom.

'H… help..' he managed and touched his chest so they'd know what was wrong.

'Oh my God, he's having a heart attack!' Hope shouted. 'Do something mum!'

'I don't know what to do. What am I supposed to do?' she asked Stephen, but he had no bloody idea either. 'You're still breathing, so I don't have to give you the kiss of life.'

Hope pulled her mobile out of a pocket and looked at it, doing nothing, just staring at it.

'999… amb… ambulance.' Stephen wanted to shout but it came out as a whisper. Thinking about it, he wasn't sure why Hope was there. She was on her honeymoon in the Maldives.

But Hope continued to stand there and look at the mobile without making the call.

'Hope… please…' He could feel himself getting weaker. The pain in his chest and arm was intensifying and he wasn't sure how much longer he could last.

No longer able to speak, he looked at Hope, pleading with his eyes. And then, as Stephen watched, his beautiful daughter began to turn black and crumble. 'You've infected me with your evil. Blackened my soul,' she said. 'I'm being sent to Hell to pay for your crimes.'

Stephen's eyes bulged as Hope turned to dust. All that was left of his precious daughter was a pile of dust which had collected in a little heap on the floor.

He looked at his wife who was still beside him. 'You bastard,' she said. 'You deserve what's coming.' Then she also turned to dust.

He was alone with two piles of dust for company. He'd lost the two people he loved the most in the world.

Now his chest was turning cold. He could no longer use his arm. It was his turn to die.

Waking from his nightmare, Stephen tried to get rid of the last vestiges of sleep, by blinking his eyes and clenching and unclenching the hand on his dead arm, to get the blood pumping again. Stephen hadn't died. He could feel his chest going up and down, so he was still breathing. But he was confused. The cold spot on his chest was still there.

He opened his eyes again and saw a figure. Dressed in black, wearing some sort of white face mask, the intruder was leaning over Stephen. The coldness on his chest turned out to be a pistol with a silencer on it, placed over his transplanted heart.

'Goodbye, Stephen,' the black shadow said.

And that time Stephen really did die.

24

The next day the book and papers belonging to Truelove were returned from forensics and Jo's team were going through them, when they began to get reports of another killing. An MP, Stephen McGrath, had been shot. The killing looked like a military style execution, or Mozambique drill, two bullets to the heart and one to the head. The gun had been left behind at the scene, but initial indications were that it would be untraceable. There was no serial number and no forensics on it at all. No blood, no skin cells, no fingerprints, nor any prints on the casings that they'd found so far.

Stood in front of the white board, where Sasha had pinned up the information they had so far, Byrd said, 'This was a professional job if ever I saw one.'

'Yes, but was there another reason he was shot in the heart? Why not just in the head? Is there more to it?' asked Jill.

'Because he was having an affair? Affairs of the heart and all that?' Jo mused.

'I've got a lead,' said Sasha, who had been peering at her computer screen.

'Sorry?' asked Jo, unaware that Sasha had been listening to their conversation. Jo was inexplicably annoyed by it. If

Sasha was going to butt in, then it better be for a good reason. But Jo hadn't minded Judith butting into conversations, so why should she mind that Sasha did it? Because Sasha wasn't Judith. Judith was dead. And Jo still hadn't come to terms with her death.

Looking at her screen Sasha continued, seemingly unaware of the fact she was getting Jo's back up. 'Stephen McGrath had a heart transplant.'

'Yes, and?' Jo couldn't keep the sarcasm from her voice.

'The newspapers picked up on the fact that he'd donated a lot of money to the cardiac department of his local hospital, to make sure he was one of the first transplant patients.'

Jo saw Crooks walking through Major Crimes and asked him to join them. 'Guv, Sasha has a possible lead on why Stephen McGrath was killed. Tell him Sasha.'

Sasha did so, but she wouldn't look at Crooks, just kept her eyes firmly on her screen. Alex looked a bit bemused by the strange behaviour, but Jo was beginning to get used to the oddities of their new co-worker. Somehow, she was finding it easier to deal with the fact that Sasha had replaced Judith, because Sasha didn't impinge on the relationship of the tight team of Jo, Byrd and Sandy. An unexpected bonus of Sasha's difficulties in interacting with people.

'So, Guv, do we get to take the case? The man was the MP for Brighton so it's within the Sussex borders.'

'Sorry, Jo, not this one.'

'Oh, OK, Guv, but why?' Jo was disappointed. 'It's linked to the Truelove case, I'm sure of it.'

'Because Brighton Major Crimes will be taking that investigation.'

'So what do we do?'

'Stay on Truelove. Whoever it is that he was dealing with are also at risk from the British Nordic League. We need to find them and offer them police protection.'

'And prosecute them for their crimes?'

'Of course, Jo. Look, I'll pass the lead onto Brighton and

Hove about Stephen McGrath.'

But watching Crooks walk away, Jo wasn't sure she believed him. And she wasn't at all convinced that any other members of Truelove's inner circle involved in shady deals with him were targets of The British Nordic League. Odin seemed to be going after members of parliament, not local councillors, at least not so far. The organ grinders, not the monkeys. But she could be wrong, and an order was an order, even though she didn't like it.

Looking back at her papers across her desk, Jo saw something out of the corner of her eye. A shadow? Someone outside? She instinctively looked over at Judith's desk and just for a tantalising moment saw her friend sat there, before she morphed into Sasha.

'I know, Judith,' Jo whispered. 'I'm trying, I really am. I'll get you justice. I promise.'

25

The team turned their attention to the photocopies of Truelove's black book. At first glance it made no sense at all. Truelove had used a code and they had to crack it. It used letters, not numbers, which made it easier. The question was, was it a complex code or a simple one? For a while the office was quiet as the three detectives poured over the pages.

'What are you lot working on?' Sasha asked.

'Trying to crack the code in Truelove's book,' said Jill. 'Not my forte really, but still…'

'Here, give me a sheet.'

Jill passed one over.

Sasha seemed to only glance at the paper before saying, 'Well that's one of the simpler codes.'

'It is?'

'Yes. It's a reflect code.'

'Uh, huh.'

Sasha still had her gaze averted from Jill. 'You don't know what that means do you?'

'No I don't. But don't make a big deal of it, Sasha, just help me out, right?'

Sasha shrugged her shoulders. She scribbled on a piece of paper the first 13 letters of the alphabet. Then under each one, she wrote the remaining 13 letters. She then put arrows going up and down between each letter.

'Here,' she passed the sheet to Jill.

'What do I do with this?'

'Dear God,' mumbled Sasha. 'Okay write the word, 'hello'. Then under each letter put the coded letter.'

Jill did as she asked.

'So, what's the coded word for hello?'

'Ah, got it now,' said Jill. 'It's 'uryyb'.'

'Great,' said Sasha, returning to her work.

Jill slunk into Jo's office and told her the code had been cracked.

Jo called in Byrd and Jill told them both about the cipher. 'Great work,' said Byrd.

'It wasn't me,' Jill confessed. 'It was Sasha.'

'I should have thought of that,' said Jo, 'and asked her to look at it. Anyway, we can rewrite the book now, so off you go.'

It was Jill who managed to identify two other people involved in Truelove's latest plan, the one which Odin was involved in.

'Got it, Guv,' she said. 'It appears to be about a large commercial development on an out of town site. Truelove was paying the head of the planning committee for West Sussex County Council and also the man holding the position of head of planning at the Chichester District Council. Any objections from local residents or environmental protesters, didn't stand a chance against the weight of Truelove's political influence and Odin's money.'

'What are the names of his cronies, Jill?'

'Harold Smith and John Jenkins.'

Byrd said, 'The book is full of deals that Truelove had been involved with. He'd even managed to buy his house outright with the proceeds going back over 10 years. Truelove was rotten through and through. It makes you wonder why he hadn't been killed before now.'

Jill watched as Jo and Byrd left the office to track down

Smith and Jenkins, feeling despondent. She would have much preferred to be out and about with Byrd, but knew she was still working a penance from their previous case. Then she'd made the grave mistake of getting involved with the Guv's main suspect and it was only her experience of psychological profiling that gave her a stay of execution.

She was desperate to remain in Jo's good books and on the team, so she was toying with the idea of doing a profile on Odin. But she'd been tasked with going through the mobile phone they'd found with Truelove's black book. Deciding Sasha would be a better fit for that task, she passed it over and pulled up her notes on Odin. Looking at her watch she reckoned that she had a couple of hours before Jo and Byrd returned, she'd better get on with it, for she wanted to surprise Jo with a profile of Odin when she got back.

26

Both Smith and Jenkins lived in Chichester, as that's where both Councils were situated. Harold Smith lived furthest from the police station, so they went for him first.

Harold Smith lived in a bungalow situated two miles west of the city in the small village of Fishbourne. It was a nice enough property, a two bedroomed bungalow on a large plot, but when you looked closely, there were cracks in the concrete drive, the front garden grass was full of choking weeds and the garage door was at a drunken angle and clearly hadn't been painted, or opened, in years.

Mrs Smith answered the door and took them through to the kitchen. 'That's where he is,' she pointed to the garden. Always pottering around out there,' she said. 'He says he's doing the gardening, not that it ever looks any better.'

Jo could only agree with the woman's sentiment, the garden's borders were a tangle of weeds and overgrown trees and bushes. And the house didn't look any better either. The kitchen looked like it had been there since the house was first built, maybe 30 or 40 years ago. There was a lean-to on the back wall that had seen better days and was slowly tipping over. The garden was long and disappeared into the distance, but again screamed old, unloved and uncared for. The concrete garden path was pitted and cracked, the grass had no edges and the fences were slowly disintegrating.

As they walked outside, Harold Smith walked towards them. He smiled and said, 'I wondered how long it would take you lot to come.'

'You lot?' asked Byrd.

'You're Chichester Police. It's written all over you two.'

'DI Jo Wolfe and DS Byrd,' Jo held up her ID and Byrd did the same. 'Mr Smith, we'd like you to come down to the station and answer our questions in relation to the murder of Sebastian Truelove and 11 other people.'

Harold Smith went white and began gabbling, 'I never killed anyone, what are you talking about? All I did was take some cash in return for a favourable planning vote.'

'What development was that for, Sir?'

Smith looked at Byrd, 'The large commercial development, just outside of Chichester. I would have voted for it, even if I hadn't been paid to do so.'

Byrd grinned at Jo. 'Over to you, Guv.'

'Harold Smith I am arresting you for fraud and for the taking of bribes pursuant to the Bribery Act of 2010. You don't have to say anything, but anything you do say may be taken down and used in evidence against you. Do you understand?'

'Yes,' he nodded as Byrd put him in hand cuffs. 'Are these really necessary?'

'Procedure, Mr Smith.' Jo wasn't giving an inch, despite the man's age. He was old enough to be Byrd's father, but that didn't mean he deserved any sympathy. She followed him and Byrd back into the house.

Mrs Smith asked how long her husband would be gone and Jo replied honestly. 'I don't know, Mrs Smith. We will formally arrest him at the station and take his statement. Then he'll go before the Magistrates. That will probably take a couple of days. I'll get someone to keep you informed.'

She squeezed Mrs Smith's hand and immediately wished she hadn't.

Jo felt the woman's pain. The blow to her jaw. The crashed fist into her eye. The breaking of ribs as she was kicked repeatedly. She looked up from the floor to see Harold Smith, eyes aflame, fists itching to hurt and control. The smell of stale alcohol was overpowering. She curled into a foetal ball and hoped it would be over soon. Crockery and glassware smashed into little pieces by her head and splinters went into her eyes and hair. Then her hair was pulled almost from her scalp. Harold was pulling his wife along the kitchen floor, telling her to fuck off and get out of his sight before he did some real damage to her.

Real damage? She looked in horror at Mrs Smith who must have seen something in Jo's eyes, for she said under her breath, 'Keep the bastard for as long as you can. I've had quite enough of him.'

Jo nodded and turned away.

***

Once Harold Smith had been booked in, it was the turn of John Jenkins. He was an altogether different animal. Younger, richer, living in a swanky townhouse complex just under a mile from the city centre. Built in the style of a mews, there was a car parking space underneath each house. Decorative bricks and pointed dormer windows adorned the front of the building and the impression was that the properties were new, smart and clean.

There was no Mrs Jenkins, just John on his own.

'Ah,' he said as he opened the door and saw Jo and Byrd there.

'John Jenkins?' asked Byrd. The man nodded and Byrd identified himself and Jo. 'Can we have a word please, Sir?'

Following Jenkins, they entered a large, bright living room. The kitchen and dining space could be seen through a break in the wall, which served to partially cut the kitchen off from the living room.

'Just going out for a run, where you?'

'Pardon?'

'You're dressed for a nice run in the park,' said Byrd and

Jo took in the man's immaculate track suit and blindingly white trainers.

'Don't be so stupid,' snapped Jenkins.

'Ah, so it's all just for show is it?' said Byrd looking the man up and down.

'Nice place,' said Jo looking around.

The giant abstract paintings on the walls weren't to Jo's taste, but she reckoned they would have cost a lot of money. As did the furniture, all New York loft living, hip and trendy, somewhat disparate from the man in front of them. John Jenkins wasn't wearing the years well. The skin on his face was taut, indicating a face lift. The hair on his head thin and wispy and Jo wondered if he was undergoing baldness treatment. The teeth were all Simon Cowell white in the orange tinged face with white eyelids and bags, meaning the tan could only have come from a sun lamp.

'Shame it was bought with funds from bribes.'

'A shame?'

'Tell him, Byrd.'

'If it is found that this house was paid for by illegally obtained funds, then it can be seized under the Proceeds of Crimes Act.'

'And do what with it?'

'Sell it to pay compensation to your victims. Fraud isn't a victimless crime, Mr Jenkins,' Jo explained. 'Think about the people who've lost their homes, who didn't get the full market value for them when you knocked them down to make way for your developments.'

'I never, I don't, I want a solicitor. Yes, that's it. I want a solicitor.'

'If you can't afford representation then one will be provided for you. But I don't think you're short of funds, are you, Mr Jenkins?'

Byrd bundled the man out of his house, making sure he didn't hit his head as he was placed in the back of their car. Jo felt that was a shame. She'd rather have had him hit it.

27

Both interviews ran along broadly the same lines.

Each of them started by denying everything, including Harold Smith, who had earlier confessed. But when they saw Truelove's black book and Jo started talking about getting search warrants for their houses and bank balances, they capitulated. They had been reduced to what they really were, weak men who had been greedy and had no morals whatsoever. They'd let down the local people in a big way. Chichester deserved better.

After taking statements, the men were remanded in custody with a visit to Chichester Magistrates Court set for the morning, and left downstairs in the cells for the night.

Jo tidied up the interview room while Byrd stayed with the booking sergeant. She picked up the black book and that's when it happened.

The walls of the interview room faded away. Jo was stood in an office, somewhere old by the looks and smell of things. It was old fashioned, small and crammed full of files and books. The old mahogany and leather desk was scratched from decades of use and the leather chair behind the desk was stained from years of the great and good using it.

But this time, sitting in it, wasn't a live human being, but a male corpse. There was something in his mouth. It looked like some sort of foam. As Jo walked closer, she could see it looked like the insulating foam builders used when renovating old properties or fitting new windows. Expanding foam that immediately hardened when exposed to the air. It appeared the foam had been sprayed directly into his throat, effectively filling his airways and causing him to die from asphyxiation.

The man's arm shot out and grabbed Jo with a strength she wouldn't have expected. 'Get him,' she heard in her head. 'Get the Nordic bastard.'

Jo dropped the book and the vision faded. It was all very well for the man to ask her to get Odin, but that wasn't as easy as it sounded. Where the hell was Odin? Who the hell was he? He was as slippery as an eel. No one had got even a sniff of a lead. She wondered what the steering committee would come up with, if anything. Sasha had identified a further man as a possible target of Odin's, based on coded information in Truelove's book. That was who had just come to her in a vision, she was sure. Time to speak to Crooks.

Jo picked up her mobile phone and called him.

'Sir, Harold Smith and John Jenkins have just been sent down to the cells for the night. One of them identified another possible target and he's in Truelove's book. It's Lord Holland. He's a member of the House of Lords and makes sure any over-arching structural development plans are passed in his chamber, those benefiting Truelove, of course. He lives in London. What should we do? Do we go and interview him, or should another team in the city do it? Whoever does it, we should be quick about it.'

'Another team will go, Jo. But why should we do it now?'

'I was just thinking that perhaps we could get someone to go to his house quickly. Tonight if possible.'

'Because?'

'If he's in Odin's sights, then who knows how quickly he'll strike? I just think the sooner the better, Sir.'

'Oh very well.'

'You'll let me know?'

'Yes. Now go away while I arrange it.'

'Thank you, Sir.'

She breathed a sigh of relief. She'd done everything she could to make sure Lord Holland was found. She feared he was already dead, of course. She never usually had premonitions, she was all about what had already happened. But you never knew, it was worth a try.

28

Jill was amazed with the information she'd found out about Odin. Figuring that if a leader of the BNL was calling himself Odin, it followed that he could have some traits of his namesake, the Nordic God of War, either by birth, or by acquisition. It would be no accident that the name was chosen.

So what about Odin that could be pertinent to the case? It was easy to see that he was a man of great contradictions. The God of War, yet the Master of Ecstasy, he was one of the most complex and enigmatic characters in Norse mythology.

He was the divine patron of rulers, but also of outlaws. A war-god, but also a poetry-god, and he was known to have prominent effeminate qualities that would have brought unspeakable shame to any historical Viking warrior. He was worshiped by those in search of prestige, honour, and nobility, yet he was often cursed for being a fickle trickster. What kind of figure could possibly embody all of those qualities at once, with their apparently glaring contradictions?

He could take countless different forms. As one saga described Odin, 'when he sat with his friends, he gladdened the spirits of all of them, but when he was at war, his demeanour was terrifyingly grim'.

This ecstasy that Odin embodied and imparted was the unifying factor behind the myriad areas of life with which he was especially associated: war, sovereignty, wisdom, magic, shamanism, poetry, and the dead.

Odin had more to do with rule by magic and cunning; a devious, inscrutable, and yet inspired ruler. He moved both male and female with his perilous gift of ecstasy, granting them an upper hand in life's battles as well as communion with the divine world of consummate meaning.

It appeared that what had happened was that he had taken Truelove to a level of ecstasy as a sexual partner, which made him vulnerable to Odin's charms. That must have been what was behind Odin's seduction of Truelove. He'd conned him into a false planning scheme, just so he could kill the man with a bomb. It was an audacious plan, yet one that Truelove appeared to have been drawn into voluntarily. Truelove had wanted more and more money. Others who fell under Odin's spell wanted more and more power, which is where the BNL came in. He was easily luring thugs and criminals into his organisation.

Whichever way you looked at it, Jill decided, Odin was a man to be terrified of.

29

At Jo's insistence, she had been patched through to the officers attending the home of Lord Holland. She was literally seeing life through a lens as the leading officer's body camera captured the scene in real time and fed the images back to the Metropolitan Police in Scotland Yard and the West Sussex Police in Chichester.

As soon as Jo saw the front door, she realised they were too late. A bright red cross was painted on the door, like a giant X. She was sure they'd find his Lordship dead.

Taking every precaution, the team entered the house slowly and silently just in case the killer or killers were still there. There seemed to be no disturbance to the house itself. Nothing seemed out of place and there was nothing obviously missing. Lord Holland had lived alone, never having married and he didn't have a partner as far as they knew.

The officers moved through the house, checking each room in turn, until they came to what appeared to be his study, located at the back of the house. Heavy drapes covered the windows and one officer moved to open them. As he pulled aside the heavy brocade curtains, he revealed an archetypal man's study. His Lordship's personal space reflected his status as a Lord. There were chesterfield sofas,

Persian rugs, portraits on the wall and right in the middle of the room a large mahogany and leather desk.

Lord Holland was slumped in the leather chair behind it. He was dead. His mouth and throat full of foam that appeared to have set, forming a solid lump effectively cutting off his airways. His eyes bulged and his face reflected his horror. He had been bound to his chair at the arms and legs by what seemed to be nylon rope. There were flecks of foam on his face and the chair, indicating that perhaps he'd tried to get rid of the foam by shaking his head from side to side, but the bruise on his temple had clearly subdued him. The man hadn't stood a chance.

30

Jo arrived at home that night, exhausted. She just about managed to climb up the stairs to her flat and once inside dumped her large tote bag on the sofa. Her phone buzzed.

'Fancy dinner?' It was from her dad.

'Sorry too exhausted to go out.'

'No, I'm bringing it up to you.'

That was a better idea. She shrugged off her coat and poured herself a glass of wine. She didn't care about what wine to drink with what food. She drunk white wine with ice. End of.

She heard her father's tread on the stairs and opened the door. He was holding a bubbling cottage pie.

'Oh, wow,' she said, as the tantalising smell reached her nose. 'Where did that come from? No, let me guess, Hayley.'

Mick grinned. 'Yeah, your sister-in-law said she was batch cooking and did one for me and one for you. It's probably more that she doesn't think either of us eat properly.'

'She's probably right,' said Jo. 'Here, put it down before you burn yourself.'

Mick put it on the hob in the kitchen.

'I'll leave it for a bit to cool down,' said Jo. 'Want a wine?'

'No, but I'll have a beer and you can tell me how the case

is going.'

And so she told him everything.

She described how she'd felt when she held Truelove's book and had the vision. How she'd watched the video feed from Lord Holland's house with growing horror. The scene was just as she'd seen it and as she'd feared, she hadn't been able to stop him being killed.

'I don't know what to do, Dad! Odin is always one step ahead of us. And we still don't really know what the bloody man looks like, nor where he lives.'

'I get this must be so frustrating for you,' her father agreed. Jo sprang from her place on the sofa and began pacing. 'How do you locate a man who exists in the shadows? What can we possibly do to lure him out into the open?'

Neither Jo, nor her father had the answer, so Jo had to be satisfied with her supper and another glass of wine.

31

It appeared someone else had been thinking over that conundrum as well and had come up with a plan to do just that. To get Odin to show himself. They were to use a senior police officer, Alex Crooks.

'You're doing what, Sir?' Jo stammered as Crooks called Jo into his office the next day.

'Well someone has to try and infiltrate the group and I've been approached.'

'But it's so dangerous!' Jo was under no illusion that Odin was the most ruthless killer she'd come across. Jill Sandy's profile of the maniac had left her in no doubt that Odin was a man to be feared.

'Well we're getting absolutely nowhere with tracing Odin, so someone has to join the British Nordic League. And that someone is to be me.'

'But…' Jo had never heard of such an absurd idea.

'It'll be fine,' Alex was obviously trying to placate her. 'They'll know who I am and what I am. I will feed info back to the committee as and when I get it and you're to be my back up. In turn the BNL will want me to tell them all about the investigation, how close we are to finding Odin and what our next moves will be.'

'Did you just say I was to be your back up?'

'Yes and the committee have approved the plan. We've got the green light. I'm to attend my first BNL meeting this evening and I'm going to offer to give them information on the police investigation, if I get a chance. I'll obviously need to come across as believing in their aims.'

The whole thing frightened Jo shitless. She knew how Odin could kill without compunction. He was driven and utterly ruthless. Pretty much as ruthless as his victims, she guessed.

'If you're really wanting to go ahead with the plan, Sir, then you'd better read this,' and Jo handed Alex a typed report.

'What's this?'

'I was just coming to bring it to you, it's like a psychological profile of Odin. It's a look at his mythological character traits and it might give you some idea as to what to be wary of.'

'Mythological,' Alex spluttered. 'Are you serious?'

Jo was confused by Alex's reaction. 'Of course, Sir. Look, you don't go around calling yourself Odin without at least admiring the original god. And if you admire him, you're likely to ape him.'

'Ape him?'

Jo wondered why Alex was being so obtuse. What she was saying wasn't that hard to grasp. 'In this report, Jill Sandy has described Odin's character. He was the God of War, but also the Master of Ecstasy. He's a man of contradictions but with the ability to draw people to him. He's slippery. You'll have to find a way of protecting yourself against him.'

'Oh for goodness sake, Jo. What do you take me for?' Alex appeared to scoff at her. 'I know what I'm doing. I'm not stupid. Now, shouldn't you be getting back to your team?'

Jo was still standing there with her hand out. Alex hadn't taken the report, nor seemed about to do so.

'Very well, Sir,' she said and turned on her heel. She'd

tried to help Alex, but her pleas had fallen on stony ground
His loss, she decided. But it didn't stop her worrying.

32

The room smelled of sweat and testosterone. Alex likened it to the smell from a male gym, all those bodies straining and competing. Wanting to lift heavier and heavier weights. Building muscles upon muscles and then seeing who could wear the whitest, tightest tee-shirt. The odours assailed his nostrils and he breathed through his mouth to try and avoid the smell.

'Name?' called a man sat at the entrance to the sports hall behind a Formica table. His bull head was shaven, and his arms adorned with tattoos.

'Crooks, Alex Crooks.' A bit James Bond-ish Crooks knew but couldn't seem to help himself.

'Is this your first meeting, Crooks? Can't say I recognise you.'

'Yes.'

'And what brings you here?'

'Well, I'm a senior police officer and I'm sick of the rich, privileged bastards getting away with their crimes.'

The man stood, towering over Crooks who wasn't a small man by any stretch of the imagination. Alex could now see why the man was on the door. He'd frighten the shit out of anyone fool enough to try and infiltrate the group, including Alex.

'Come with me.'

They walked along the length of the hall, which was rapidly filling full of jostling, male clones and an air of menace hung over them like a pall. Crooks was taken to a room near the stage.

'Let me see your ID.'

Alex supposed the man meant his police ID and duly passed it over.

'Chief Inspector, eh? A big fish no less. Well, Chief Inspector, you have a problem with our legal system, do you?'

'Like I said, I'm sick of the rich and privileged getting away with stuff.'

'What's made you think like that?'

Alex pushed up the sleeves of his rugby shirt. It was getting hot in the small room and Alex was beginning to feel claustrophobic. Trying to put a tinge of anger in his voice he said, 'Well it all started with the MP's expenses scandal to be honest. And it's gone downhill from there. I'm sick and fed of up identifying those with criminal intent, only to be shut down because of the 'old boys club'. You'd be surprised how rife it is, even down here in leafy Sussex.'

'Hah, even more so down here, mate. Lots of them live out here in the sticks in their country houses or weekend cottages. Go back into the hall and enjoy the show. Come back in here after and I'll give you these back.'

Alex was somewhat perturbed to see his badge and ID card being pocketed by the giant in front of him, but as he wasn't in a position to do anything about it, he just nodded and slipped out of the door. He guessed they'd use the time to check him out, which was fine. Thank God for real covers and not fake ones.

The hall was now crammed full of bodies, all jostling for position. Alex had expected it to be like a male-only club for the working class, but there were women there too with a fervour in their eyes that matched their male counterparts. He felt an air of danger as people turned to look at the newcomer, but for the most part they left him alone. Some nodded a decidedly unfriendly hello, others looked him up and down with a sneer. Not the most welcoming bunch, Alex decided. Perhaps it was just their natural reticence. You're no one until your face has been seen around a few times.

The scrutiny of him ceased as a large screen rolled down on the stage from an overhead gantry. The lights dimmed and the show began.

33

It appeared that there was a live feed coming from what looked like the interior of a church. There was a figure striding around and the camera followed him, but he was always in shadow and his features couldn't be seen. Apart from his hair. Long and corkscrewed, it flew around the man's head as he spoke. Alex couldn't see what colour his hair was as the feed was in black and white. Strange. But Alex figured it was done to maintain anonymity.

'Comrades. I'm sorry I'm not able to be with you in person tonight, but I have urgent business here in London, which is why I'm speaking to you from our headquarters.'

'Heil Odin, Heil Odin,' rang around the hall and every man and woman held out their right arm, fist clenched.

Crooks was jostled as people realised he wasn't joining in, so rather self-consciously, he raised his fist as well.

On the screen, Odin held up his hands and waited for the adoring chants to fade.

'My message to you tonight is one about corruption. Contrary to popular belief, corruption is not specific to poor, developing, or transitional countries. In western countries cases of bribery and other forms of corruption in all possible fields, exists.

'They can take many forms. Under-the-table payments

made to reputed surgeons by patients attempting to be on top of the list of forthcoming surgeries.' Crooks knew all about that one and so did the audience as, 'Heil Odin,' rang around the room again. Crooks lifted his fist with the others this time without being prompted and found a few people were now beginning to nod at him. There didn't appear to be any compassion for the dead MP from Brighton, rather just fanatical adoration for the man who had ordered the kill.

When the chanting died down again, Odin continued, 'Bribes are paid by suppliers to the automotive industry in order to sell low-quality connectors used in safety equipment such as airbags. We've identified bribes being paid by suppliers to manufacturers of defibrillators to buy their low-quality capacitors. Other sections of society aren't immune from this, either. There are financial and other advantages granted to unionists by members of the executive board of a car manufacturer, in exchange for employer-friendly positions and votes. The examples are endless. They must stop. We will make them stop.

As, 'Heil Odin,' once more rang around the room, Crooks fancied he could hear echoes of other halls in other parts of the country, from the live feed.

'Up and down the country, cases exist against members of various types of non-profit and non-government organizations, as well as religious ones.

'Ultimately, the distinction between public and private sector corruption appears rather artificial, and national anti-corruption initiatives will be needed. So, Northern England, are you with me?'

The hall in Sussex stayed silent and they all heard the chants from the live feed coming from another hall.

'The Midlands are you with me?' Odin shouted.

The audience around Crooks were beaming with pride and fervour.

'The West Country?' Odin was roaring.

'The South of England?'

That was the cue the people around Crooks had been waiting for. 'Heil Odin,' they chanted and it was screamed from every voice, as his followers were determined to be the loudest and fiercest part of the UK.

At the end of his whistle stop tour of Great Britain, Odin finished with,' We will defeat them, the elitists ruling classes. We will tear down their castles, swim their moats and set fire to their treasures. For we are the many and they are the few. Together we are stronger. Together we are a force for change that is already sweeping the country. They will not defeat us. They will kneel at our feet.'.

The roar that filled the hall was ear splitting. Everyone around Alex was displaying the fervour of the converted. It reminded him of the terraces at football matches, the centre court at Wimbledon erupting when Andy Murray beat Djokovic in the final, the triumphant return of the England cricket team bearing the Ashes. Only this time the crowd were not celebratory, they were baying for blood.

34

By the end of the meeting, Crooks was drained. Wet through, his hair was plastered to his scalp and he was pretty sure he was very red in the face. As all the rest of the members of the British Nordic League turned to leave the hall, Crooks slipped back through the door into the private room, expecting to see the doorman and his goons. It was empty.

Fuck.

His ID was not something you lost or gave away. Ever. The bollocking he'd receive for that could get him demoted. He stepped outside the room, back into the hall and looked around wildly. Then he spotted the doorman. By the door. Of course. How bloody stupid of him. But it just showed how high his anxiety levels were.

He walked over, trying to look nonchalant but was sure he'd failed when the man grinned at his arrival. 'You looked a little upset there, Chief Inspector. Looking for these were you?'

And there was his ID card and badge. In the man's meaty paw. Alex felt like falling to his knees and begging the man for them, but instead stood there resolute.

'Here you are,' said the bouncer, 'and here's details of our next meet. Oh and there's going to be a rally soon in

London. We're organising transport from all corners of the country. Maybe there'll be a chance for you to meet Odin there.'

'I'd like that,' said Alex. 'I'm sure I could be very helpful to him, what with my insider knowledge and all.'

'Exactly, that's what he's hoping as well. But let's just take it slowly, OK.'

Alex nodded his agreement and took his ID and badge. 'Until next time, then.'

'We're looking forward to it, Chief Inspector. Very much.'

Even what on the surface could be taken as a welcoming turn of phrase, was said with undertones of menace.

Once back in his car Alex drove a little way away from the sports centre and then parked up in the shadows. His hands were shaking too much to drive and he had difficulty in lighting a cigarette. But he thought on balance that he'd passed muster. It was natural that he would be eyed with suspicion. Why should they trust him? He'd have to prove himself, he was in no doubt of that. He just wondered what the price of that proof would be.

And then a few days later, the answer fell into his lap. The word from the ACC was that the two politicians involved with Truelove and the bribery scandal were not being prosecuted. Good news for Crooks, but first he'd have to tell Jo.

35

As Alex feared, the news didn't sit well with Jo. He'd called her into his office to tell her first thing that morning.

'I'm sorry, Jo,' he said. 'Word has just come down that the two politicians in cahoots with Truelove are not being prosecuted.'

Jo stood looking incredulous. 'Why not, Sir? Bloody hell. I knew this would happen.' She began pacing up and down in front of his desk.

'They say there isn't enough evidence.'

'Who does?'

'The CPS.'

'What? The buggers confessed! How can the Crown Prosecution Service take that view?'

'Smith and Jenkins have redacted their statements and so now the CPS aren't going forward with the case. It all hinged on the confessions. Without them we don't have much of a case at all. There's no paper trail. There's no trace of any money because there wasn't any. The briefcase held a bomb not cash.'

That's when Jo really lost it, and he couldn't blame her. 'Oh for fuck's sake. Apart from a lack of prosecution, don't they realise how much danger these people could be in? If we let them back on the street, Odin can get to them for sure. He went after Truelove. We have to believe he'll go after the councillors. You told me that yourself. You were the one campaigning for us to find them. Bloody hell, how could you let this happen, Boss? Just who's side are you on?' She banged down her cup onto Alex's desk.

He stood and went to her side. He put his hands on her arms and turned her to face him. 'Look, Jo, sometimes these things happen. There might be something going on that's above our pay grade. A wider investigation. A new way forward. Who knows? Ours is not to reason why. Getting angry about it won't change anything.'

The fight went out of Jo. 'No, I know, Boss. Sorry. It just galls, you know?'

Alex did know. It had happened a few times to him during his career. It's just that this time Alex was pleased about it. Jo was right. The two officials were in danger. From him. For they were to be the scapegoats. Crooks was going to serve them up on a silver platter. To Odin.

He suddenly had an urge to hug Jo. He pulled her to him, relishing in the feeling of her slim body resting against his, the hint of strawberry coming from her short hair. He was just about to burrow his nose into it when she went stiff and pulled away.

'What the hell?'

The look of horror on Jo's face told him he'd made a major faux pau. But in his defence, he found her so tempting, he always had. There was nothing wrong in that, was there? After all they'd been close at one time. All he wanted to do was to regain that intimacy.

Shrugging away his confusion at her rejection of him, he wasn't worried. Now he'd made the initial overture, he was sure they'd become close again soon.

36

Byrd approached Alex Crooks' office just at the wrong time, or the right time, depending upon your point of view, he decided. Alex Crooks had his hands on Jo's arms and she was looking up at him. What the? Did it mean anything? Don't be stupid, he told himself. Jo wouldn't a) be that stupid to fall for her boss and b) cheat on him. At least he didn't think so. Didn't hope so. Oh fuck. He wanted to turn and run away. Pretend he'd not seen that moment of intimacy, but he had news and had to go in there, break up their little tête-à-tête.

In the end, he was glad he had gone in, because as he entered the office, he could see that Jo was actually scowling up at Alex, and not looking in the least enamoured by Crooks' hands on her arms. She took a step backwards, causing Crooks to let go of her and turned and smiled at Byrd.

'Eddie, what can we do for you?'

'News, Boss. Not good I'm afraid.'

'Shit, another death?'

Byrd nodded. 'Judge Chambers found dead in his chambers, of all places.'

He could see Jo stifle a smile. 'And who is Judge

Chambers?' Alex Crooks asked and moved back behind his desk, looking at his two subordinates.

'A bit of a do-gooder by all accounts,' said Byrd. 'Had a reputation for lenient sentences, so career criminals would fight tooth and nail to get him on the bench for their case. He believed in reforming criminals and would let them off with lighter sentences if they said sorry.'

'Sorry? Did you just say, sorry?'

'Afraid so, Boss. He also liked a kick-back in return, mind.'

'What happened to him?' asked Crooks.

'He was found hanged in his chambers in Winchester Crown Court. The killer had left a note to say that he had been tried in the court of the British Nordic League, found guilty of taking bribes and sentenced to death. They said the sentence reflected how justice was done before Britain became soft and repealed the death penalty. This is what we've got so far,' he handed Crooks a file.

'Thanks, Byrd.' Crooks opened the folder. Then closed it again. He looked up, 'This won't be anything to do with us, as the killing took place in Hampshire, so I suggest you get on with… um… whatever it is you are doing.'

Jo and Byrd looked at each other askance, then left as requested.

Eddie put his hand on Jo's arm and stopped her in between floors.

'What's wrong?' she turned and smiled up at him. The smile that he'd come to know. And quite possibly love. Whatever, it was definitely not the look she'd just given Crooks.

'Nothing,' he said. 'Nothing at all. '

37

Later, alone in the ladies' toilets, Jo could finally relax and try to make some sense of what Alex had done to her in his office. On the surface, putting his hands on her arms hadn't been that bad, she supposed, but pulling her towards him and hugging her? That was a big no no. She hoped she'd made that clear by her actions and her expression. Thank God Byrd had come in when he did, forestalling any further advances from Crooks. But would he repeat his advances? And how far would he go next time?

It looked like she was heading back to a situation where Alex would continue to touch her, feeling that they had 'a connection'. It was bad enough last time when he'd been married. But this time he wasn't. There wasn't that barrier anymore.

It made Jo feel helpless, something that she wasn't happy about. She needed to be able to feel comfortable at work, whether her colleagues were male or female. Alex Crooks was making her feel decidedly uncomfortable. And what's more, Byrd could have easily got the wrong impression about her and Alex, when he walked in on them. And that would never do. She did think he'd seen something, though. It was the way he looked at her in the stairwell, as though he were seeking validation that nothing had happened with

Crooks, nor was it likely to.

Of course, she had the option of going to Human Resources and make a complaint about Crooks. Report him for sexual harassment in the workplace. But the big fear there was if it would endanger her career, or help it? She thought the staff in Human Resources would be fine about it. That she'd be believed and that both Jo and Alex would be treated fairly. However, what about her other colleagues in the station? Particularly the male officers? Would they be as understanding? She was sure Alex had his cronies, all of whom could make her working life very difficult indeed.

On the other hand, it could show Crooks and his outdated mates in the station that she meant business and that they should all stay away from her. But then she could feel isolated. Oh, all she was achieving was going round and round in circles. For the moment, she'd leave things as they were. But if he tried anything again, she'd review the situation then.

38

The central message at the next meeting of the British Nordic League was what the League stood for. This time upon his arrival, Crooks was greeted by name and with a handshake from the bull-headed bouncer on the door.

'Good to see you back with us, Chief Inspector. Odin was hoping you'd join us once again. Enjoy the meeting and be sure to say goodbye when you leave.'

Alex nodded and moved away, up through the throng to be nearer to the stage. He wanted to glean what he could from the pictures being beamed into the hall. To find any clues that might lead them to Odin's lair.

But first, the 'Heil Odin,' chants rang out, raising the blood pressure of everyone there, filling them with a fervour you didn't often see in the modern world which relied on electronic communications, not huge gatherings. It was usually only pop concerts that attracted so many zealots. Or Trump rallies, Alex had to concede.

And then there was Odin, filling the screen with his larger than life figure and persona. Crooks wondered if this splitting up into factions of the faithful was deliberate. For Odin appeared to them all almost as a God, or demi-God, his huge physique filling the screen, larger than life, dominating the hall.

He began to speak once the shouts had died down.

'People ask who are the British Nordic League? What do we do? What do we stand for? Well I guess the general answer is that we are fascists. What is fascism? A form of government that is a one-party state. No more flittering around with which party has the biggest majority. No more working out who is an MP on the take. No more working out who is in whose back pocket.

'Some might say that fascists are against democracy. We're not against it per se. It's just that we believe that a one-party state is the best form of government. The British Nordic League would make sure the country was prepared and ready at all times for armed conflict. Ready, willing and able to respond to economic difficulties. For we put nation and race above the individual. If the British Nordic League were in power, there would be a centralized government. But all governments need a figurehead. A leader.

'British fascism has a long and exalted history, being formed in the 1920's around the time Italy became ruled by the first of the fascist leaders, Benito Mussolini and then in Germany the Third Reich was formed under Hitler.'

Alex thought that the comment about the British fascists was definitely up for debate, after all Mosely and his black shirts didn't get very far into the public conscience. The people of Great Britain were facing being taken over by Hitler and if they had anything to do with it, it wouldn't happen. Quickly Mosely found himself on the wrong side of public opinion and that was the end of the British fascists.

But Odin was on a roll now.

'Who do you want to be your leader?'

A rhetorical question, but Odin asked it anyway, just so the crowd could shout, 'Heil Odin. Heil Odin. Heil Odin.'

Hot, sweaty and exhausted at the end of the rally, Alex filed towards the exit at the end of the hall. He hadn't gleaned anything from the live feed. He couldn't see any equipment driving it. He couldn't get a hold on where Odin was broadcasting from. He wondered if he was ever going to make any progress.

'Ah, Chief Inspector,' said the bouncer at the exit. 'I hope you enjoyed tonight's show?'

Alex just nodded, as his throat was raw from all the shouting. After all, he had to look like he was becoming a devotee and join in.

He accepted the man's handshake and was then slipped an envelope.

'There's some details for you of our next meeting. There's to be a great rally in London on Empire Day, the original date in March. Fitting don't you think? Odin should have time for you after that is over. And you've been added to the membership of a private Facebook group, where Odin and the central committee members post updates. Just apply to join and you'll be admitted. See you in London.'

Alex once more nodded, stuffed the envelope in his pocket and followed the others out into the cool night air. Moving away from them, he found a quiet spot and leaned back against the wall, dragging oxygen into his lungs and letting the night air cool his sweaty face. At last he was making progress. And thanks to the CPS he had a gift for Odin when he met him in London. He loved it when a plan came together.

39

While Alex was at the BNL rally, Jo was holed up in her apartment, chatting to her father. She had just told him about the death of Judge Chambers and gone to the fridge to refill their drinks.

Coming back, she said, 'I didn't have a vision of his death. I hadn't known about that one until Byrd told me.'

As she handed Mick his beer he asked, 'How's things with you two?'

'Me and Byrd? Okay I guess.'

'You guess?'

'Yeah, it's just that Byrd seems to keep touching base with me.'

'Sorry?'

Jo sat back down on the settee. 'Oh, you know, little chats in stairwells, lingering a little longer when we're parting, asking about Alex quite a lot.'

'Ah well, there you have it.'

'I do?'

'Yes, he's jealous.'

'Jealous? But there's nothing to be jealous about!'

'Isn't there? You were close to Crooks once.'

'Well I'm not now and I'll thank you to keep out of my love life, dad.'

'It was you that brought the subject up,' Mick laughed. 'But seriously, is Crooks bothering you?'

'Some, I guess.'

'Some?'

'He put his hands on my arms and tried to hug me the other day. Nothing much.'

'That's nothing?' Mick took a long pull of his beer.

Jo realised her dad didn't think much of Alex's actions. 'It's not that bad,' she said, trying to deflect from how bad it really was.

'Jo, he shouldn't do it at all. It's the 2020s not the 1970s. You should report him.'

'And how's that going to go down, eh?'

'You need to have faith in the system, Jo.'

'Well, maybe after the case is over. Anyway I need to get ready. Byrd is coming over for dinner,' Jo stood and collected Mick's empty bottle.

'Ah, my cue to leave I take it.' Mick prised himself out of the chair. 'Cooking are you? Only I didn't see any food in the fridge.'

Jo grinned. 'No, as you well know I don't really do cooking. Byrd learned that to his detriment. He's bringing a takeaway with him. Now push off and let me get ready.'

40

It was a week later when Alex travelled to London to go to the Hyde Park rally. It was turning out to be an uncomfortable experience. He looked and felt out of place, despite wearing a rugby shirt and jeans. It seemed that everyone else wore tight t-shirts and his trainers were definitely not white enough. Also, and possibly worse, he'd bought them from a discount store and there was no branding on them.

There was a heavy police presence, all in uniform, with backup from dog handlers and mounted police. From what he could see there were plain clothed police in the crowd as well. They looked as out of place as he did. It would be just his luck if one of them recognised him and wondered why he was there. Hopefully they'd just think he was on the task force (which he was) and infiltrating the crowd as his colleagues were.

The irony of the location wasn't lost on Alex. Speakers Corner at Hyde Park was a national institution. It was where people could congregate on a Sunday morning and talk about any subject under the sun. Speakers Corner was located on the north-east edge of Hyde Park, nearest Marble Arch and Oxford Street. Historic figures such as Karl Marx, Vladimir Lenin and George Orwell were known to have often used the area to demonstrate free speech.

The other irony was that close to where Alex was standing, about 250 years ago, people were still being hanged at the infamous Tyburn Gallows. The gallows were installed in 1196 and by the time they were dismantled in 1783 more than 50,000 people had been executed there. He wondered if Odin had plans to restore the tradition.

Everyone condemned to die at Tyburn could make a final speech. Some confessed, others protested their innocence or criticised the authorities. For onlookers, executions at Tyburn were big social events. Londoners could buy a ticket to watch the executions from a seat on huge wooden platforms.

Eventually, the authorities decided the hangings were too rowdy and transferred them to Newgate Prison. But the tradition for protest and pleasure in Hyde Park continued.

Alex estimated there were already thousands of people there. He wondered if they were all devotees. But there were probably many sceptics around to see if Odin could persuade them. He worked his way nearer to the stage, where he met the ubiquitous door man. Alex's hand was shaken and then he was led into the VIP ring at the front of the stage. He tried to keep a low profile, he didn't want to admit who he was to random strangers, so he avoided talking to anyone.

When Odin came on stage there was a ring of security around him, burly men dressed entirely in black. They fanned out and stood at the front of the stage, some facing out, some facing in. Odin stood higher than them on staging, so he could be seen by his adoring fans. Once again, thanks to the big screens, he seemed larger than life. He reminded Alex of a mix between Steve Jobs and Donald Trump as he worked the crowd and gave them the message they'd come to hear. However, they still wouldn't be able to identify him. For Odin was wearing a beanie hat and a white face mask. One of those that reminded Alex of The Joker. All smooth features and high black eyebrows, moustache and goatee. It was disconcerting, listening to the man's message, but not being able to see who the man was. He could have been anyone, but the crowd seemed to accept that they were listening and watching their great leader, Odin.

Basically Odin threatened that hell, fire and damnation would rain down on anyone taking advantage of the state. Corrupt, lying officials needed to quake in their boots, for the British Nordic League was coming. They would all be found. They would all be exterminated like the filthy vermin they were.

He also went on about Empire Day, which took place on various dates, but latterly on the 2nd Monday in March. Although not officially recognised as an annual event until 1916, many schools across the British Empire were celebrating it before then.

Each Empire Day, millions of school children, from all walks of life across the length and breadth of the British Empire, would typically salute the union flag and sing patriotic songs like Jerusalem and God Save the Queen. They would hear inspirational speeches and listen to tales of 'daring do' from across the Empire, stories that included such heroes as Clive of India, Wolfe of Québec and 'Chinese Gordon' of Khartoum.

In Britain, an Empire Movement was formed, with its goal to promote the systematic training of children in all virtues which was conducive to the creation of good citizens. Odin reminded the crowd that those virtues were also clearly spelled out by the watchwords of the Empire Movement; responsibility, sympathy, duty, and self-sacrifice.

Empire Day remained an essential part of the calendar for more than 50 years, celebrated by countless millions of children and adults alike, an opportunity to demonstrate pride in being part of the British Empire.

With a final flourish, he reminded people that the British Empire was no longer a major force in the world, but he intended to change that and bring pride back into our country and our history.

'Are you with me?' Odin asked.

Of course they were, and they showed their solidarity as, 'Heil Odin' rang around Hyde Park. Crooks fancied that Winston Churchill was turning in his grave about then.

At the end of the rally, Alex filed out of the VIP area but was stopped by the bouncer and taken left behind the stage, instead of turning right with the exiting crowd.

Weaving through the maze of light gantries and cables, they emerged outside to where a Winnebago was parked. There were two security men by the door, plus one at the front and one at the rear of the vehicle. Alex was patted down and checked for wires. Only then was he allowed in.

Inside was gloomy. Alex was prodded in the back by a security man who had climbed in with him and who stood close behind him. In front of Alex, lounging on the settee, was Odin. The space was small, made smaller by three men inside it. Maybe that was the reason that in the flesh Odin was striking, even more striking than on the big screens, for now there was perspective, Alex against Odin.

The man looked like a cross between the Gods Thor and Odin rolled into one (at least according to recent cinematic releases) but it was the best analogy Crooks could come up with. He was large, larger than life and strikingly beautiful. Alex was surprised he was being allowed to see Odin's face, but now that he'd seen it, he couldn't believe that anyone could be so beautiful. He was in awe of Odin's charisma and was amazed that he'd been selected to see the God in the flesh and to look upon his face. It was like a religious experience. Alex was turned into a devotee before you could say, 'Heil Odin'.

'Chief Inspector, so glad you could come.' The voice of Odin seemed to reverberate around the small space and hurt Alex's ears, but then that could just have been the tinnitus caused by the music that had blasted out of the speakers all afternoon.

'I was considering how you could best help us in our righteous quest.'

Alex was still speechless. Now he'd got used to it, the voice seemed lyrical.

'As you are a senior member of the police force, I thought you might have a gift for me?'

That shook Alex out of his stupor, and he remembered why he was there.

'Yes, yes I do. Two compatriots of the MP Truelove that aren't being prosecuted, although they're as guilty as sin.'

'And who are they?'

Alex handed over an envelope. 'You'll find all the details in there.'

Odin took the envelope and looked back at Alex. He had the most mesmerising eyes Alex had ever seen. They seemed all seeing, all powerful. They made him want to help this man with a God's name, help him in his quest to rid Britain of the corruption that was rife in the UK Government.

'Thank you, Alex,' the man purred. 'I won't forget this act of friendship on your part. It shows me you were willing to listen to our ideals and found that you agreed with them. You do agree with me, Alex, don't you?'

'Oh yes, yes I do,' said Alex and surprised himself by realising that the statement was true. Above all else he had a desire to help and to please this man.

Odin tapped the envelope. 'If this information turns out to be true and rather valuable, then I'm sure we'll meet again. Would you like that, Alex?'

'Yes, yes, Odin I would. I'd look forward to it.'

'In the meantime, then, can you cast about for any other fish that would fit well on our hook? Would you do that for me, Alex?'

'Yes, of course. I'd be glad to.'

'Good. We'll speak again, soon.'

Odin nodded to the bouncer still stood behind him and Alex was rather rudely pulled out of the motor home. But it didn't seem to matter. No slight did. Not anymore. For Odin had smiled upon him and that had changed everything.

41

It was Oliver Prendergast's first assignment at University, where he was doing a teaching degree. He'd poured over the question. It was about a way of teaching mathematics, which to be honest sounded double Dutch to him. He'd tried to ask others from his class what the question meant and how to answer it, but as he'd shunned most of them upon his arrival, deeming them to be socially beneath him, his request fell on deaf ears. Why should they help an over-privileged, under-educated toff who couldn't stand them, until he needed them? He had to admit he wasn't very good at this whole education thing. He had everything money could buy, apart from those elusive little grey cells. Maybe someone should invent a way of making stupid people more intelligent? The problem was he had no idea how it might be done.

It was still a shock to him that he'd managed to get into university at all. Maybe the Dean was a friend of his father's? Who knew? None of that was his problem, really. A more pressing one was what to do about the bloody assignment? He guessed he had no choice but to try and answer it himself. He'd much rather be down the pub. One trip to the Student Union had been his last. At least down the pub one could have a civilised drink, chatting to other like-minded drinkers, not wading ankle deep in spilt beer and drinking cheap vodka disguised as Smirnoff.

He pushed his dark, unruly but straight hair away from his face and tried very hard to concentrate on the books laid out before him. But it didn't help. He examined and then cleaned his nails. He changed the radio station. He looked around his room thinking he really should tidy up and possibly even do some washing. But he still didn't understand how to work the washing machines. Perhaps he'd just take everything to the laundry in town. Or back home with him next weekend. Mrs T, the housekeeper, would be glad to get someone to do it for him. He checked his phone for missed messages, but there were none. He wondered what was trending on Instagram, or Twitter, but he'd turned the internet off, precisely so he wouldn't get distracted. Oh, it was no good. Maybe Olivia could help.

He rang his twin, who was doing an English degree at the same university. But she couldn't help either, merely pointing out that as she was studying English, what the hell did she know about teaching mathematics?

'Honestly, Oliver,' her plummy tones came clearly down the line, 'I'm having enough trouble myself, thank you very much. Most of the time in class, or in study groups, I haven't got a clue what anyone is talking about. It's as though they've read different books to me. Really, do they all have to swan around talking about esoteric this and metaphors for that. The best metaphor I'd been able to come up with was that the woman in the book who drank red wine all the time, was secretly wishing it was blood.'

'Oh,' said Oliver, not knowing what else was expected of him.

'Well, I can tell you that that nugget didn't go down very well and there was lots of raucous laughter about vampires.'

'Oh dear, poor you,' Oliver managed, thinking that just maybe she was having a worst time of it than he was, if that was at all possible.

'I've kept my mouth shut since then. So no, I can't help

you, Oliver. End of.'

He didn't even have the opportunity to ask her once again, pretty please, as she'd put the phone down.

Oliver sighed. It seemed Olivia was in as much trouble as he was. Oh well, maybe they'd scrape a Third and then move back to the country pile and run the family estate. In his opinion the whole charade was a load of bollocks.

42

The following week, Jo and Alex were sat in the Task Force meeting and Alex was being quizzed on the subject of the BNL rally in Hyde Park.

'Did you have a meeting with Odin?' the chairman of the committee wanted to know.

Alex shook his head. 'No, sorry, Sir. It wasn't for the want of trying, mind.'

'So you don't have any more information that could help us identify him?'

'Not a thing, Sir, my apologies.'

'Did anyone manage to glean any information from the rally as to the identity of Odin?'

'No, sorry, Sir,' said the ACC of the Metropolitan Police. 'I had a lot of officers in the crowd, but no one saw any more than the rest of my men, only the beanie hat and the bloody face mask. Who the hell is this joker?'

Jo wanted to snigger at the faux pau wondering if it was intentional. It was clear to everyone that Odin was wearing what most of them were describing as a joker's mask. The trouble was she didn't think he was a joker and neither did any member of the Task Force. They knew how dangerous the man was and how imperative it was that he was identified and found. They seemed no nearer than they had

114

been from the moment the BNL was identified as being behind the explosion in the restaurant. That seemed a very long time ago now, although it was only a few short weeks.

The meeting was washing over her. She vaguely remembered Alex saying that his request to meet Odin had been denied, but that he was still hoping to make a breakthrough.

The meeting then went on to discuss ways of taking Odin down. The general consensus was that they were right in not storming the stage and arresting Odin in front of thousands of onlookers during the rally in Hyde Park. They had no idea if his minders were carrying guns, they were fearful of rioting and, to be honest, they didn't really have anything to arrest Odin for. Maybe inciting public unrest (which there hadn't been), making racial slurs (he hadn't really done that anyway) and, of course, murder (which they definitely couldn't prove as Odin would simply say it wasn't him). In fact no one could prove that the man on stage was really Odin, as no one knew who he was, or what he looked like. Only his inner circle, Jo guessed, and they couldn't find, or identify, any of them anyway.

Jo's mobile buzzed and she slid it off the table and looked at the message. It was from Byrd. The body of Harold Smith had been found by his wife. Jo closed her eyes. She'd been right. She hadn't wanted to be, mind you. She'd warned Crooks this could happen. The man might have been on the take and a wife beater, but it didn't mean anyone had the right to take his life. He should have been prosecuted and served a sentence. She passed her phone to Alex.

After he'd read the message, he asked the chairman to excuse them and Jo slipped out of the room with him.

Once outside Jo desperately wanted to remind Alex that she'd told him this would happen. But he was her superior officer and talk like that would likely mean he could suspend her for insubordination at the least and pull her off the case at the worst. So she just looked at him, her eyes filled with anger at yet another senseless death.

'We'd better check on John Jenkins as well,' she said.

Crooks just nodded.

'Are you alright, Boss?' Jo saw he'd gone really pale with beads of sweat breaking out on his face. Then the penny dropped. He'd known this would happen. But how?

Alex nodded. Then he grabbed her arms again, a gesture Jo was beginning to get really pissed off with.

'Thanks for your support, Jo,' he said. 'I really appreciate you being in my corner and helping me with this under cover shit. Get back to your team and let me know about Smith and Jenkins.'

'Yes, Sir,' Jo said and stepped backward in an attempt to get Crooks to let go of her. But he didn't.

'Perhaps we can meet up tonight and you can bring me up to date on the case,' he said.

Before Jo could say that wouldn't be a good idea, he'd gone back into the Task Force meeting.

43

Jo texted Byrd to meet her at the Harold Smith crime scene. They pulled up at his house at the same time. Pulling on protective clothing, they threaded their way through various police vehicles and signed in at the door to the house. The door with the big red cross on it.

'Who reported the incident?' asked Jo.

'His wife.'

'We'll talk to her afterwards.'

Byrd nodded his agreement. 'This way, Boss,' and he led the way into the living room.

The metallic smell of blood, lots of it, filled Jo's nostrils as they walked into the room. In the middle, facing the television, was a dining room chair. Tied to it, was Harold Smith. He was wearing one of those horrible white masks with black eyebrows, moustache and goatee.

His forearms were resting on the arms of the chair and tied to it at the elbow and hand. It wasn't tied at the wrist, as that was held upwards, so the inner part of his arm was exposed and accessible. The skin had then been slit lengthways along the vein. On both arms.

'Jesus,' said Jo. 'That would have been a horrible, lingering death, watching your own life blood pump out and not being able to do anything about it.'

'Someone must have really hated him,' agreed Byrd.

'Have we got an approximate time that this was done?'

'Jeremy thinks around 3 am.'

'Who found him? The wife?'

Byrd nodded. 'It was this morning, when she came downstairs. She rang 999 as soon as she found him.'

Jo squatted down and saw that Harold's ankles had been tied to the chair leg and his torso tied to the back of the chair.

'I expect that was a bit of a shock,' said Jo.

'For him or her?'

'Both.'

'Come on, let's go and see Mrs Smith. Where is she?'

'Being looked after by a neighbour.'

'Come on then, let's get this lot off and go and see her.'

A woman with red eyes and wild hair opened the door to them.

Byrd identified themselves and asked to see Mrs Jenkins.

'Yes, of course, she's in here,' and the neighbour led them indoors.

Mrs Smith was sat on a settee. A tv was on, with the sound down, showing the news presenter reporting her husband's death. The neighbour sat down next to her.

'I'm sorry, but we need to speak to Mrs Jenkins alone,' Byrd said. 'Perhaps a cup of tea?'

The neighbour nodded and scurried away, closing the door behind her.

Jo took the neighbour's place. 'I'm so sorry for your loss, Mrs Jenkins. What a terrible shock it must have been.'

'To put it mildly,' she said. 'It was horrible, just horrible.'

'Do you have any idea how the intruder got in?'

'It must have been through the patio doors, they were open when I came down, I left them like that so you could see. I just ran to the phone and dialled 999 and then ran upstairs to quickly put some clothes on. I'd only just come back downstairs again when your officers arrived.'

'And you didn't hear anything?'

'No, nothing at all.'

'There's no damage to the patio doors that we can see,' said Jo.

'Perhaps it was someone Harold knew, and he let them in?'

'Yes, that's possible,' she agreed.

Mrs Smith dabbed at her eyes as though she were crying, but Jo couldn't see any fresh tears.

'You look very pale, Mrs Smith. We'll leave you for now, but I'll come by later and let you know what's happening.'

'Thank you, Inspector.'

Once outside, she asked Byrd to go and talk to Bill and ascertain how long the forensic examination of the scene would take. Jo then suited up once again and went back inside the house. She needed to look at the body again before Smith was taken to the mortuary. She wondered if there were any sign of a struggle? Or other injuries that might tell her something?

Once there, she walked around Harold Smith's body, studying it from all angles. There was nothing to indicate a struggle. Perhaps he'd been drugged. Jo didn't think a person would allow someone else to bind them to a chair and slit their wrists. She'd have to make sure Jeremy did a full tox screen. Jo knelt down and as she reached out to feel the rope tying Smith to the chair, the sleeve of her plastic suit rode up and her arm accidently touched the side of Harold's bare arm.

Harold Smith was still alive, just. He'd regained consciousness and found he was tied to a chair and his wrists were bleeding. He had a memory of someone claiming to be a friend of Trulove's, with an important message. He'd thrown caution to the wind, in the hope of still getting some money out of the whole debacle and let the man into the house through the patio doors. He remembered very little else and had a bad headache. He struggled but found he just didn't have the strength to try and pull his arms or legs out of their bindings. Getting old sucked. Nothing worked like it should anymore, including his muscles. Mind you the knots in the rope felt pretty solid and they didn't seem to have any give in them at all. Squirming around wasn't helping, it just increased the blood flow as his heart beat quickened. The blood from his slit wrists was dripping onto the floor. He could see they'd both been cut along the vein, not across it, so at least he'd die sooner rather than later, he supposed.

Then he heard a footstep on the stairs, as the wood creaked and groaned under someone's weight. Harold sighed with relief and his eyes filled with tears. It must be the wife. She'd ring for an ambulance and untie him. Perhaps bind his wrists so he didn't lose much more blood before the paramedics arrived.

She walked into the living room and stopped by the door. Her gaze roamed over the chair, him and the blood. Dear God, thought Harold, there was so much blood. She'd have to be quick.

'Help, call an ambulance and then untie my arms, we have to stop the bleeding.' He wasn't sure if she'd understood, his voice was muffled due to some sort of mask over his face.

Instead of leaping into action as she should have done, he watched in astonishment as she turned her back on him and left the room. The phone was in the kitchen, perhaps that's where she'd gone. He strained to hear her voice, but there was only silence. What the hell was she doing? He called to her again and again, his voice getting weaker with every shout. But got no reply, the only noise was the creak and groan from the wooden stairs as she walked back up them.

She'd never said a word. Just left him to die. Alone and in pain.

Jo stood when the vision faded and looked around the room. She wasn't sure how she felt about Mrs Smith's actions. On the one hand she couldn't blame her as he was a wife beater. Plus, she wouldn't necessarily have been able to save her husband's life. But on the other, he was still a human being and deserved better. Was Mrs Smith guilty of an offence? Jo wasn't an expert but guessed it would come under 'omission' i.e., Mrs Smith omitted to help her husband, when she could have. But Jo couldn't prove any wrongdoing by his wife. The pair had been alone in the house as the murder had been perpetrated in the middle of the night. Anyway, as Jo couldn't tell anyone about the vision, no one else would know what Mrs Smith had done, or rather hadn't done.

44

Jill had gone to John Jenkin's address with another member of the wider investigation team, Ken Guest. Ken was nearing retirement age, a fully paid up member of the police black humour brigade and was an experienced Detective Constable, who had never felt the need to rise up the ranks. He was a, 'hit the ground running' kind of man and proud of it. Jill always felt it was like working with your dad, partnering Ken, but she didn't mind. She was inexperienced and he was very experienced. She could learn a lot from him.

They knocked and knocked at John Jenkin's mews house but couldn't get a reply. Didn't really expect one, what with the big red cross on the door. Questions of neighbours led them to believe Jenkins was inside, so they went through the neighbour's house to the back of the plots to gain access. Luckily it didn't entail climbing over a 6-foot fence as the houses only had small walls between them. Looking over the brick wall they could see the patio door of Jenkin's house swinging in the wind.

'That's not a good omen,' said Ken.

'I thought there were only bad omens,' Jill said.

Ken smiled. 'You know what I mean.'

Jill nodded.

'Come on, let's go in.'

Jill shivered at the thought of finding a dead body. She hadn't much experience of that and quite frankly didn't want to. But then again, being a detective, she supposed she had to get used to it.

'I'll go first,' Ken said, 'follow on behind,' and he easily climbed over the wall.

Jill nodded and kept close to him.

It wasn't difficult for them to find John Jenkins. He was sat in a wooden chair, facing the patio doors and could easily been seen through the window. They were sure he was their victim, despite his face being covered by some kind of white mask. There was a large pool of something black on the floor beside both of his arms. Jill got a little closer, then promptly ran to the corner of the garden and threw up.

'You alright, Jill?' called Ken from inside the house.

'Fine, thanks,' she said although she was feeling anything but.

'You need to call Jo,' he said. 'Tell her about Jenkins and don't forget the fact that he's wearing some sort of mask.'

'Mask?' Jill had been so focused on the blood, she hadn't looked up at the victim's face.

'Yeah, reminds me of that Joker bloke. I'm taking pictures with my mobile. And then call Bill, we need forensics out here toot suite. I'll get hold of Jeremy.'

Jill pulled a tissue out of her pocket and wiped her mouth, then popped a mint in it. She took a deep breath and grabbed her mobile to call the boss. She couldn't wait to get back to the office, but knew she'd be at the scene for several hours. Sighing, she pulled up Jo's number and pressed the green call button.

45

The four detectives met back at the office and gathered around Sasha's desk, who was flicking through the crime scene photographs sent through by Bill. They were displayed on her monitor.

At the end, Jo said, 'Both deaths were very similar and in both cases a joker's mask was left.'

'For goodness sake, that's not the face of the Joker,' said Sasha in her usual abrupt fashion.

'Oh. What or who is it, then?'

'A 'V for Vendetta' mask.'

'A what?'

'V For Vendetta. It's a film made from a graphic novel. It's set in a dystopian future and a mysterious person called V rescues a young girl called Evey. He wears this anonymous mask.' Sasha's clipped tones brooked no dissent.

'Right. So not the Joker then?'

'No. I've just said that.'

Jo shrugged. Either way the mask was androgynous and a clever disguise. The face painted on the stark white background drew the eye and turned your line of sight away from any other features such as hair, hands, clothes. You became fixated on the mask, just as she was doing. She supposed the masks were placed on the victims to reinforce the point that Odin had ordered the killings, just in case the red blood on the door wasn't enough.

'This is a new thing,' she said. 'We know that Odin wears this type of mask to disguise his identity. Now he's publicly claiming his kills at the scene, not just via the press or social media, but owning it with these masks. It's to taunt us.'

The other four must have agreed with her, because no one said anything. They were all looking at the mask which filled Sasha' screen. Jo felt she'd proved her point. And it made her bloody angry.

46

Jo was still annoyed when she returned home that night. As Mick climbed the stairs to her flat, she was banging about in the kitchen.

'Hey,' he said rubbing her back. 'Calm down, what on earth's wrong?'

'Bloody Odin,' she spat. 'He's getting under my skin.'

'That's probably what he wants.'

She had to agree. Jo turned away from the sink and looked at Mick. 'He's killed two more people. He's taunting us. His mask has been left at the scenes. I don't know what to do,' she finished, her outburst spent.

'Sit,' Mick ordered and put the kettle on. Not until he'd handed her a herbal tea did he sit opposite her and say, 'Right, start at the beginning.

Haltingly at first, Jo told her father what Odin was up to. She believed he was leaving the masks to taunt the police. To taunt her.

'Why?' Mick took a gulp of his coffee. 'Why would he taunt you. What do you think he's trying to say?'

'To tell us he's better than we are. To show we're no good at our jobs because we don't have a single lead to follow. He's really starting to piss me off.'

'I'd never have guessed.'

Jo glared at him. Then had to laugh at his po-face. 'And you can stop winding me up as well.'

Mick smiled. 'You do realise this is what Odin wants?'

'What?'

'You, wrong footed, unable to move forward. Stuck, right where he wants you.'

'And how the hell am I supposed to move forward then? Tell me that.'

'You have to channel that anger into solving the case,' Mick said. 'Not let it become all-consuming, for then you'll not get anywhere. Don't obsess over your anger, climb above it and get on with working the case. It's just a mind fuck.'

'It's certainly that,' she had to agree.

'Anyway, I don't think Odin does the killing.'

'No?'

'No. He'll have people in his organisation to do it for him.'

'So I have to firstly prove who has done the killings. Then prove that the order came from Odin himself.'

'Yep.'

'Shit. See, I told you it was a mind fuck.'

47

The long tables in the Early Education Unit of the university were filled with students preparing to get their assignments back. The air in the room was charged with excitement, but Oliver felt only dread. He'd just about managed to answer the question, he felt, and had poured over his books well into the night. Well until 10pm when he'd fled down the pub before last orders. He'd done a couple of pretty looking graphs and taken at least three words to describe something when just one would have done, otherwise the bloody thing would have been too short. Whoever heard of producing 3,000 words on strategies for teaching maths to little kids? Who the hell could even do it?

He'd got the paper in, just, by the deadline and now they were about to get the results. The lecturer, a stern woman who was the last person Oliver thought should be a teacher, was calling out names and handing sheaves of paper over. That made Oliver realise that whatever he'd done, whether it was right or wrong, he'd not done enough of it.

The volume of chatter was rising as people congratulated each other at their grasp of the concepts and A's were flying all over the room. A couple of the students had gotten B marks from what he could see, but as far as Oliver was concerned that was worth a celebration in itself. Didn't they realise how lucky they were?

Oliver was last to receive his paper. Of course he was. At least old dragon breath (Oliver's rather unkind name for her) had done him a favour and not embarrassed him in front of the class. When he was handed his paper there was a large 'D' written in red pen on the top of it. Shit.

'What do you think you did wrong, Oliver?' the dragon asked.

'I don't know, I'm afraid,' he answered truthfully. 'If I did know, I would have done that and not what I did, don't you think?'

Even Dragon Breath had to agree with that. She took a few minutes to try and explain what he should have done, but even that went over his head.

'Can I try again?' he asked. 'Now that you've helped me.'

Her steely gaze said it all.

'I guess not,' he mumbled and slouched off, thinking perhaps scraping a Third was a bit optimistic.

When he phoned Olivia that night, she'd had a rough old time of it too.

'Honestly, Oliver, I've no idea what the hell people are talking about most of the time. Why couldn't we have stayed at home after A levels? I'd much rather be in the stables, than here.'

'Because father wants us to get university degrees.'

'But why? What purpose does it serve when we're clearly not cut out for higher education?'

'Appearances, my dear. Every generation of the family ad infinitum have gone to university, so we must do as well.'

'Oh, alright. Anyway I'm really looking forward to going home next weekend. Are you still coming?'

'Wild horses wouldn't stop me, sis.'

'Wild horses is just what I'm looking forward to,' said Oliva. 'I'm hacking out with Sophia. Can't wait.'

48

Against her better judgement, Jo agreed to meet Crooks for a drink that night to discuss the case. He said they'd be able to speak more freely away from the office and anyway it was good to get out and get away from the austere building they worked in. They agreed to meet at 7pm. Jo didn't go home before hand; she went straight from work and didn't put any make up on. Petty, but the last thing she wanted was for Alex to think she'd dressed up for him.

Alex stood as she entered the pub and called her over to a small table tucked away in one corner. The place was pretty empty, it being that strange hour between the after-work crowd leaving and the out for the night punters arriving. He'd already bought her a white wine. She had been about to order a lime and soda, so she wasn't very impressed. However, she didn't want to upset him, so she sat down, pulled the glass to her, but only took one sip.

He began a desultory conversation about work, but it didn't take long for him to turn the conversation to more personal matters.

'You know I've always liked you,' he started. 'Had feelings for you. Let's face it, Jo, those feelings broke-up my marriage.'

He reached across the table and covered her hand.

'Don't you have anything to say about that, Jo?' Alex looked imploringly at her.

She'd never understood Alex's pursuit of her, as he'd known it wasn't reciprocated. She'd told him that many times. And she was just about to tell him again.

'But, Alex, you know I don't feel the same. I never pretended otherwise. The last thing I wanted was to be the reason your marriage broke up.'

'And you weren't the reason? How can you say you weren't?'

'Because it was the job that did that, Boss. And you know it, if only you'd be honest with yourself. At the time, you were looking for some comfort, a bit of excitement, of happiness even and you thought I was the one to give that to you. But that isn't who I am, Alex.'

He looked crestfallen.

'It's nothing against you, but you're my boss and there's not that… that… spark.' Jo didn't know what else to say.

'It's okay. I understand.'

But he clearly didn't. He cleared his throat, tossed back his wine and stood. 'I think this is my cue to leave,' he said and stalked out.

When the barmaid came to the table, Jo realised the bastard hadn't paid the bill. She quickly settled it and left the bar, deliberately going in the opposite direction to Crooks. She mulled over the feeling that the more distant she tried to be the more Crooks made out he needed her. Did he really? Was he just trying to pull her into his arms? Or was he trying to get her onside, should the whole bloody case blow up in his face?

49

The following morning, Byrd stopped Jo in the stairwell.

'Morning, beautiful, you okay?'

Jo smiled. She loved the way Byrd made her feel all tingly inside. Why did she ever think that cutting herself off from people, not letting her emotions take a hold, was the right way to live? It had been mostly self-preservation, but still, life was much more fulfilling with a partner by her side.

'Where were you last night, then? Out on the town?' His face smiled, but it didn't meet his eyes.

Oh God. Here goes. Jo took a deep breath and told him the truth. 'Crooks wanted to meet, ostensibly about the case.'

'But?'

'But he started on about how much he liked me and that I was the reason his marriage failed. He says his wife picked up on his feelings for me.'

'And?'

'And what? I turned him down flat, Byrd. Of course I did.'

'What if he keeps on? Keeps trying?'

'He's not going to do that. I gave him no room for doubt.'

'This isn't the first time, though, is it?'

Jo had to admit that it wasn't.

'See I told you. If he tries anything on in my hearing, I'll… I'll…'

'You won't do anything, Byrd. You'd lose your job. Look, if he does it again, I'll report him, I promise. Or ask for a transfer. Something. Anything. Come on, Eddie.'

But she could see Byrd didn't like it. His body language was giving him away. His fists were clenched and there was that muscle thing going on in his jaw. She'd never put him down as the jealous kind. Why wasn't he believing her when she said that Alex meant nothing to her?

'Look I can't talk to you when you're behaving like this,' she said. 'Get over yourself. Anyway, don't you have any work to do?'

As soon as the words were out of her mouth, she regretted them. Byrd became very still and his eyes narrowed into a piercing hostile stare. He spat, 'Yes, Boss,' then turned on his heel and stalked away.

Jesus Christ. What was she to do? She'd been honest, told him how she felt about Alex's advances and that she would take positive action if he didn't stop. What more was she supposed to do? She stomped off to the canteen to get a coffee.

She had already been pissed off with Alex and now she was pissed with Byrd. Why did men have to complicate things so much? Honestly, they talked about men not understanding women, but she was damned if she understood men.

Maybe she should kick the whole Crooks and Byrd thing into touch. Ask to be reassigned. But she daren't do that, it could kill her career. But would this nonsense kill her relationship with Byrd? She didn't want it to.

As she queued for the coffee, she mulled the problem over. Tried to see it from all angles. People said hello to her, but she didn't hear or see them. She was consumed by her internal struggle. Alex had put her in a position where she was fighting for her right to love and have a relationship with someone of her own choosing. She wouldn't throw away that right. She'd continue rebuffing Alex. But would she report him? She didn't know. The jury was still out on that one. For now, she'd try and get Byrd back onside. When he got over his hissy fit that was. But she knew she shouldn't have snapped at him like that. She hoped he'd get over it. Soon.

50

The British Nordic League
Making Britain a better place for the British.

Today I want to talk about corruption. The British Nordic
League are against corruption in any form.
Forms of corruption vary, but include bribery, extortion,
cronyism, nepotism, parochialism, patronage, influence peddling, graft,
and embezzlement. Corruption may facilitate criminal enterprise such
as drug dealing, money laundering, and human trafficking, though it
is not restricted to these activities.

What really interests the BNL is misuse of government power for
other purposes. For instance, repression of political opponents.
General police brutality is also considered political corruption.

Over time, corruption has been defined differently. In a simple
context, while performing work for a government or as a
representative, it is unethical to accept a gift. Any free gift could be
construed as a scheme to lure the recipient towards some biases. In
most cases, the gift is seen as an intention to seek certain favours such
as work promotion, tipping in order to win a contract, job or
exemption from certain tasks. And what about cases of junior
employees giving a gift to a senior manager who can help propel the

*junior up the promotion ladder? Or Parliamentary Private
Secretaries who give their government masters gifts for similar
favours?*

*So you see, corruption has many guises. Do not fall prey to any of
these. And if you suspect someone in your organisation is corrupt,
then tell us! Do not bother with the police, history tells us they will do
nothing.*

*But the British Nordic League?
You can count on us.*
ODIN

Rosamund Prendergast closed her paper as the butler entered the drawing room, with two cut glass glasses and a decanter full of Bristol Cream sherry.

'Oh, thank you, Stephen,' she said. 'Anywhere will do.'

The butler placed the tray on the mahogany cabinet that ran along the wall of the sitting room, nearest to the door. He then served Mr and Mrs Prendergast with their drinks, before silently retiring from the room.

'Come on, St John, put the paper down, we need to discuss the twins.'

'What? Oh, alright,' he said and roughly folding The Times he did as his wife asked.

'I'm worried about them,' she began.

'Aren't you always?' In truth St John was getting rather fed up with these 'little chats' with his wife about the twins. The hour between the close of the working day and the start of the evening, was the time of the day he liked best. It was his time to read the paper or catch up on the news, and he was irritated that his wife was interrupting it.

'I'm afraid that they're struggling.'

'Struggling?' St John's brain wasn't working tonight, he was still thinking about the in-depth article about farming that he'd just been reading. St John wasn't a stupid man, but he was focused. The only thing that really mattered to him was the estate and the smooth running of it. Oh and there was the small matter of profit, let's not forget that. Although it was getting harder to keep them in profit each year, at least not without selling the odd bit of land at an inflated price to one of his cronies.

'Yes, they're finding the work hard at University. Olivia has been on the phone.'

'That girl's always on the phone to you. Anyway, it's your fault she's there. I told you the twins would struggle at University, no matter which one you picked.'

'I didn't think English literature would be a problem.'

'It is if you don't like reading books. Olivia isn't you, Rosamund. You can get through several books a week. But her? Not a chance. How's Oliver getting on?'

'Just as badly, I'm afraid.'

'So your very expensive plan hasn't worked then. I don't know, they cost me enough in back handers to get them there and now you seem to think you've done the wrong thing. We better change the subject before I get really cross and say something I shouldn't. Now, have I told you about the new sheep breeding programme we're about to embark on?'

As St John pontificated about his latest money-making scheme, he was filtering out his worries about the twins. Oliver and Olivia were their only children and were as thick as two short planks. Rosamund had cost him a fortune when she'd insisted on greasing the wheels firstly of a marker of A level papers and then Deans who were kind enough to let the twins study at their university. Promises of new libraries were potent persuaders, he'd found. And now it looked like it had all been for nothing.

51

Jo awoke with a start. She looked around the bedroom but could see nothing amiss. It must have been the smell that woke her, she decided. Smoke. That was it. That's what she could smell. Smoke that clogged up the hairs on your nostrils, filled your sinuses and then irritated the back of your throat. But there was no clamour of smoke alarms. Byrd mustn't be able to smell it as he was still deeply asleep, lying next to her on his front with his head turned to one side, facing away from her. At least he was there, after the dreadful thing she'd said to him. She'd eaten humble pie and apologised as soon as she left the canteen. He'd come round last night to talk about stuff, but they'd gone to bed instead. A much more satisfactory way of clearing the air, than long drawn out discussions.

She started to climb out of bed to open a window and let some fresh air in, when the frame and glass began to shimmer. What the hell? It was fading in and out, just like in a Dr Who episode when the Tardis appeared at a new location. Only this time it wasn't a phone box that materialised, but Judith.

'What? Judith? Is that you?'

A stupid question, of course it was Judith. She knew what her friend looked like - she'd been killed by a bomb, with tattered clothing and frizzled hair. Wet through with water from the firemen's hoses.

'Jo, you must defeat Odin. It's imperative. He's an evil spirit, taken human form, to ensure that the Vikings will rise again.'

'Vikings?' Jo was a bit confused, which was understandable considering her bedside clock said it was 3 am and Judith had been dead for weeks.

'Yes. He is planning an unholy war against all non-fascists. His power is great. He shouldn't be underestimated.'

'What's with the Fascist shit?'

'All will bow to Odin as their leader. He's growing in influence and is going to be a UK Mussolini, Hitler or Franco. Like the black shirts in the 1930's, before the war.'

'Are you sure?'

'Yes. It's real. It's frightening. He must be stopped.'

'But how?'

But it was no good. Judith was fading for real this time. She opened her mouth, but Jo couldn't hear what she was saying. Mind you, her warning had been stark enough.

Jo laid back down and closed her eyes but tossed and turned for the rest of the night thinking about Judith.

Did she really appear? Was she real? Or was it a nightmare? Was it really Judith warning her? Or was it Jo's active imagination working through problems in her dreams.

The 7am alarm clock awoke Jo with a start and Byrd began to stir beside her.

'Morning, beautiful,' he said pulling her towards him.

Then he abruptly sat up. 'Jo? What's that smell?'

'What smell?'

'Like something's burning.'

'Oh, that,' Jo laughed. 'I got up earlier because I was hungry and burnt the toast. It's nothing to worry about,' and she kissed him, hoping to allay his fears.

But it had confirmed hers.

Someone or something really had visited her last night.

52

All that day Jo thought about Judith. If she had to face the fact that the visitation during the night was real, how the hell was Jo going to defeat Odin? She hadn't got the faintest idea. Finally giving up on the pretence of working, she packed her tote bag to go home. She could sit there and go through her copy of the files. Perhaps a change of scenery would help her concentrate.

'Sasha,' she said, 'if anyone wants me tell them to call my mobile. I'm going home, I think I've a migraine coming.'

Sasha nodded, which Jo took as an affirmation.

'You alright, Boss?' said Byrd.

'Yes,' Jo nodded. 'Just not thinking straight today.'

'Fair enough.'

'I'll see you tomorrow,' Jo said and surreptitiously squeezed his hand.

He nodded his agreement.

Jo was relieved. Putting Byrd off coming over that night, would allow her the time and space she needed to talk to her dad.

She arrived home around 4pm and this time went into the main house to see him. She found him in the lounge, a laptop on his knees, facing the immaculate garden.

'Not gardening today, Dad?'

'No, too wet. All it will do is provoke my arthritis. God, I hate getting old. All I seem to talk about is my aches and pains. Anyway, enough about me. Coffee?'

Jo nodded.

'Good and then you can tell me why you're here, back from work so early. Come on.'

Jo followed her father into a kitchen/diner which would comfortably fit her flat into. It had recently been remodelled, with shiny white cabinets and black marble work surfaces. Jo sat on a bar stool and looked around.

'This is truly stunning, Dad.'

'Thanks. I still can't believe it's our kitchen.'

Jo owned half the house with her father and so they'd re-mortgaged to fund the cost of replacing the old kitchen, which had been in place for about 20 years.

'You did a great job of project managing this and the new extension.'

'Thank you, but that's not what we're here to discuss,' he said, placing a cup of coffee in front of her.

'No, I know, it's Judith. She came to warn me about Odin last night.'

'Ahh. Our raping and pillaging Viking.'

'Yes. She told me I should be frightened of him. To take his threat seriously. She said something about him being an evil spirit.'

'Did she now?' Mick joined her at the kitchen island, sitting opposite her.

'You don't seem surprised.'

'I think you should go and see Keith Thomas. You've been putting it off for long enough. I'll come with you, if you like.'

Jo paused for a moment, then sighing, 'Alright. It's Wednesday, so he'll be at the Church. If you call him, I'll drive. Come on,' she said and walked back into the lounge, grabbing her coat and bag.

Keith Thomas ran the local Spiritualist Church and Jo had seen him when she had the first experience of being able to find out what had happened to the dead when she touched them. But with this case, her gift had broadened into also seeing those spirits who were confused and angry about their death and refused to 'pass over' to the other side.

The moment Jo walked into the Spiritualist church she felt calmness wash over her. They'd missed the service, but to be honest Jo wasn't into that side of spiritualism. Listening to visiting mediums wasn't her cup of tea and therefore she'd not gone to another service after her first. But the man who ran the church was a different matter. Keith Thomas was her spiritual mentor.

He'd been performing healing on a couple of church members and when finished, he motioned Jo forward.

'Oh, no, Keith, I'm fine, really.'

He stood, resolute.

'Oh, alright.' Jo walked reluctantly to the massage table and climbed on it.

Keith began with making sure his hands were warm enough by rubbing them together and then passed them over her body but without touching her. Whilst he was doing this, the warmth from his hands felt as though Jo was sitting in front of an open fire, with a storm outside. He then began laying his hands on her head. Her stress headache began to drain away and by the time he'd finished, she was smiling. But he wasn't done. He then moved his hands to her stomach.

It was like having a warm hot water bottle placed to help stop cramps from period pains, or colic. All the pain from the bomb explosion was stored in her stomach and as she let go of it, she began to cry. Just a few tears at first, which slid silently from her eyes, but after a few minutes she was well and truly sobbing, so Keith moved one hand back to her head. She started to calm down, the sobs stuttered and then stopped, the hitching breaths subsided and her eyes fluttered closed.

She wasn't aware of how long she'd been lying there when she came around and Keith helped her off the table.

'Feel better?' he asked.

Jo nodded. 'Much, thank you, although that wasn't the real reason I came.'

'Yes it was,' he said, 'you just didn't know it. So what else is bothering you?'

Jo told him about seeing Judith repeatedly and then the warning in her last visit. 'What I want to know is if you think it's really Judith I'm seeing. And do you think she was right about Odin? You know, the whole being an evil spirit thing?' Jo could hear the doubt in her voice, but just couldn't stop it. 'What do you think? Can you explain it?'

'For me,' Keith began, 'it's all about the continuous existence of the human soul. The creative force, or energy of a person cannot be destroyed; it merely changes its form. Spirit, as part of the creative force is, therefore, indestructible. And so, on the death of the physical body, the spirit continues as an integral part of the spiritual world.

'And seeing Judith?' prompted Jo.

'The spiritual world penetrates this material world,' Keith spread his hands, 'but in a different dimension. I believe that in spirit life, we have a spirit body, which, until we progress far enough, is a replica of our earthly body. Individuals in the spirit world remain the same individuals with the same personalities and characteristics.'

'Don't they fully 'pass over' then?'

'That's one way of looking at it. Individuals in the spirit world only progress through their own efforts. Individual personal responsibilities do not stop at death, therefore Judith keeps appearing to you because she would have been an integral part of the team who are jointly responsible for stopping Odin.'

'So you think Judith will stay around until we get him?'

'If that is what you believe, because of what you know about her personal traits, then yes. She won't progress until the job is done. She must believe it's her personal responsibility to help the investigation. To help you. To stop Odin.'

'Thank you, Keith. This whole visit has made me feel so much better about myself and my abilities. And that healing, I can't begin to describe how much that helped.'

'You should come more often. At least when you're part of a big investigation.'

Jo smiled. 'I will, but let's hope there aren't too many of those.'

53

Oliver and Olivia travelled home together. It was early on Saturday morning when they arrived in Oliver's Alpha Romeo, just because there was more room in his car for their copious amounts of washing. Neither had classes on Monday, so they were looking forward to a three-day break, being cosseted by their housekeeper, Mrs T, who also used to be their nanny.

Oliver flew down the long tarmac drive to the house. Being winter there were no paying guests tramping through the public rooms and so Oliver could park outside the main door. They both climbed out of the car and stretched as though they'd been in there for hours, when in actual fact the house was only a 30-minute drive from Portsmouth.

Mrs T had obviously heard Oliver's sliding stop which had been accompanied by much squealing of rubber and she flung open the door to greet them.

'Hello my lovelies. How marvellous to have you home at last.'

Olivia ran up for a hug and Oliver said, 'Stop being so dramatic, Mrs T. You saw us last weekend!' at which all three of them fell about laughing.

They tumbled into the hall and made for the kitchen. Stephen, their handyman, come butler, come chauffer was dispatched to get their bags and put them in their respective bedrooms, while Oliver and Olivia were treated to strong black coffee and the aroma of breakfast being cooked and bread being baked.

Olivia sighed with happiness and Oliver agreed with her sentiment. It was as if the old house had wrapped its arms around them. They were home. They were safe. They could forget about university and its pressures for three whole days. Imagine!

'Are mother and father up yet?' asked Olivia.

'I haven't heard them,' said Mrs T.

'I'll go and get them,' said Oliver and scraped his chair back to leave the table.

'Wait for me!' called Olivia and together they raced up the stairs to their parent's bedroom.

Without stopping they bundled through the door calling, 'Mother, father, we're home,' in unison.

'Come on,' said Olivia.

'Get... get...' said Oliver, the rest of his sentence dying on his lips.

And then Olivia began to scream.

54

The next deaths fell squarely in Jo's patch. It was early Saturday morning and she was revelling in a rare lie-in with Byrd, as neither were on duty. She was considering getting up to make coffee, when her mobile pinged. As did Byrd's. They looked at each other, both knowing what that meant.

'Shit,' said Jo and reached for her phone.

'Fuck,' said Byrd and reached for his.

Both had the same text message. 'Emergency call received reporting two deaths at Putnam House. Suspected homicide.'

Neither of them needed an address. Putnam House was sufficient.

'Shit,' said Jo again and climbed out of bed.

Byrd grabbed her arm and pulled her in for a last kiss.

'Now you can get up,' he said with a grin.

They drove to the estate in separate cars. Jo arriving first and Byrd following on. But they had stopped at a drive-through to buy much needed take-away coffees. Jo was pretty sure their relationship was becoming an open secret, but they still liked to keep up appearances. That included not arriving at a murder scene, early in the morning, together. Professional decorum and all that.

Byrd joined her on the steps of Putnam House. He

looked around and whistled. 'How the other half live,' he whispered to Jo, just before the door was opened by an obviously distressed woman.

'Hello,' Jo said. 'We're from Chichester Police,' and she and Byrd held up their ID badges.

'Thank you for coming so quickly,' the woman said as she moved away from the door to let them in. 'I'm Mrs Treadstone, the housekeeper, otherwise known as Mrs T.'

'Could you tell us what's happened?' Byrd asked.

As they spoke, Jo could hear crying coming from another room, but it was hard to know which one, there seemed to be many doors leading off the vast hallway they were standing in. There were black and white tiles on the floor, wooden panelling on the walls and a rather grand carpeted staircase sweeping upward.

'The children arrived home from Portsmouth, went to wake their parents and… and… oh dear,' Mrs T rocked backwards, and Jo grabbed her elbow before the woman fell. 'They're dead. Both dead,' she said.

'Could you show us, please?'

Mrs T nodded and recovering with the aid of a few deep breaths, led them up the sweeping staircase to the next floor, and stopped at the first door on the left.

'In here?' Byrd asked.

Mrs T nodded, then with great effort said, 'I'll be in the kitchen with the children.' She turned and fled back down the stairs her footsteps dulled by the thick carpet.

Jo had no idea where the kitchen was, but that wasn't her priority. They had to see what was behind the door.

The smell was the first thing to reveal itself. As Jo pushed open the door, it rushed out to greet them, making them gag. As the door continued to swing open, Jo walked in with Byrd right behind her.

A large bed dominated the room.

Two dead bodies dominated the bed.

A man and woman, both with their throats slit, lying naked on their bed. They wore androgynous masks on their faces, which were stark white, with sweeping black eyebrows, moustache and chin.

'V for Vengeance,' mumbled Byrd.

There was a note pinned to the headboard and they moved to either side of the bed to read it:

St John and Rosamund Prendergast, liars both, corrupt and without shame, laid bare for everyone to see.
ODIN
British Nordic League.

'St John? What sort of name is that?'

'It's pronounced Sinjun.'

'Sounds bloody pretentious to me,' said Eddie and Jo couldn't disagree.

'We need to get Bill and a team here as soon as possible and pathologist. Ask for Jeremy. You know the drill, Byrd. And make sure uniforms are on their way.'

'Yes, Boss,' he said, all trace of their earlier intimacy wiped away. This was work and they were focused and professional.

Byrd left the room to make the calls and Jo stood with the dead couple for a few moments. She had no idea what they'd done to attract the attention of the British Nordic League, but was sure they'd tell her soon enough in the mortuary.

For now, she had to meet the children.

55

As Jo walked back down the sweeping staircase, she heard cars arriving and Byrd ordering the troops. Uniformed police were dispatched to stop anyone entering at the front entrance and another Jo put at the door to Mr and Mrs Prendergast's bedroom. Jill arrived and she was dispatched to interview the staff. Jo assumed the best way to find them would be the servant's entrance, although she had no idea where that was.

After several false starts, Jo found the entrance to the kitchen, only to find that Mrs T and the children had retired to the breakfast room. A young girl who seemed to work in the kitchen, at least she was wearing a white apron, showed Jo where it was. Jo was getting seriously disorientated and felt she had walked onto the set of Downton Abbey. Putnam House was something else. Stately, sedate, plush and more. It was an amazing place to visit, but Jo couldn't imagine living there. It was too cold and impersonal.

She pushed open the breakfast room door and found Mrs T and two other adults sat at a table covered in the crispest white linen Jo had ever seen.

'Oh good, you found us. We thought it would be quieter in here. Can I get you a tea or coffee?' Mrs T stood and walked over to a cabinet covered in silver dishes, coffee pot and tea pot.

'A tea would be nice, thank you.'

She sat at the table and Mrs T placed a cup of tea in front of her.

'Milk?'

'What? Oh, yes, thank you.'

Once Mrs T had finished fussing, Jo looked at the other two sat at the table. 'How are the children taking it?' she asked.

The two looked up, puzzled. Jo immediately saw two things. The first was that the pair were quite possibly identical twins. It was uncanny how much alike they were considering one was male and one female. The second thing was that she'd made a mistake assuming that they weren't the children everyone was talking about.

'Oh, I'm so sorry,' she spluttered. 'I'd assumed, I mean…'

'These are the children,' said Mrs T. 'Oliver and Olivia. They found their parents dead on the bed.'

'I'm DI Jo Wolfe,' Jo introduced herself. 'I wonder could you tell me a little about yourselves?'

It emerged, haltingly, that they were both at Portsmouth University, although studying different subjects. They came home as much as possible as they didn't seem to fit in there, being more interested in country pursuits rather than alcoholic ones and most definitely not educational ones.

'I like to ride,' Olivia said.

'Oh, so do I,' said Jo, glad to have found something in common with Olivia at least.

'Do you have your own horse?'

'No, unfortunately not. My job entails being out for hours on end, and sometimes days,' said Jo thinking of the bomb and shivering, 'and being called out in the middle of the night. I couldn't regularly look after an animal. It just wouldn't be fair on either of us.'

'If you'd like to ride out, one day, I'd love to show you the estate.'

'You have your own horse then?'

Olivia nodded. 'I've a stable of six. I wanted to study equestrian husbandry, breeding, you know, that sort of thing. But father insisted on English. God knows why,' she wiped a tear.

Jo thought Olivia could do what she wanted now but kept that nugget of information to herself.

'We'll have to take over the running of the estate,' said Oliver rather sadly. Jo couldn't immediately put him as the sort who could take over such a responsibility. Oliver and Olivia looked both young and heartbroken.

'What are you studying?'

'Education,' he said. 'God knows why. Father said he wanted to encourage school tours and all that entailed, so he made me enrol in the course at Portsmouth.'

'Why are you unhappy there? Is there any other reason?'

Both twins nodded. Olivia hung her head then mumbled, 'We're not very brainy. Much better at messing around on the estate.'

'God knows how we passed the GCSE's and A levels,' said Oliver.

At that point Mrs T shushed Oliver and said, 'I think that's enough for now, Inspector. The children have had a terrible shock.'

'Yes, yes, of course. Thank you for your time, all of you. Oh, one last thing, will you give us permission to go through your parent's things, papers, laptops, banking information?' Both twins looked blankly at her. 'It is normal investigative procedure. Otherwise I'll have to get a search warrant which would delay everything. In a murder enquiry time is of the essence.'

Both looked to Mrs T for guidance. At her slight nod they both agreed.

Jo passed each of them her card. 'If you think of anything that could help, please ring, would you? Any time night or day. You'll also be allocated a family liaison officer who will keep you informed of the investigation's progress and pass onto me anything you or she thinks could be helpful. Right, I'll see myself out.'

Jo fancied Mrs T had wanted to stop the twins talking about their lack of educational prowess earlier. If that was the case, Jo had an inkling of what could be at the root of this investigation. Bribery and quite possibly fraud.

56

Back at the station they all watched the video from the CCTV footage that Sasha displayed on her large monitor, so they could all see it at the same time. Jill and Sasha sat behind their desks with Jo and Byrd perching on the edge of an empty one. Sasha had also isolated the part they were interested in. It was a bit like being in the pictures, waiting for the main event to start and Jo smiled at the memory of Saturday mornings with her brothers in the local picture house.

The video started and Jo leaned forward. A black dressed, black footed figure with a black duffle bag over his or her back. The masked figure tapped at the servant's entrance door. It opened as though by itself, so whoever opened it could not be seen. The figure slipped through without looking back.

A mere 10 minutes later according to the time stamp, the figure re-emerged. Once again, the tape didn't show the identity of the conspirator. The black figure blended into the night, presumably having found a suitable entrance to the estate, perhaps over a part of the wall?

'Play it again, Sasha and this time we can talk about what we see.'

As the CCTV ran again, Jo asked, 'What do you reckon,

a man or a woman?'

'It's too difficult to see, Boss,' Eddie said. 'Everything's bloody black!'

'There's clearly a contact inside the house.'

'Agreed,' said Jo. 'There was no forced entry, no alarms going off. It had to be an inside job, it's the only thing that makes sense. Who was awake at that time of night to let our murderer in?'

'How did the person get in and out of the estate? Isn't there a large wall all round it? And locked and alarmed gates?'

'I'll get uniforms to go all round the estate's perimeter. See if we can find the entry point. There might be footprints, tyre tracks, rubbish left lying around.'

'It's so frustrating,' said Jill. 'It's highly likely that the figure is the killer, but there is absolutely nothing to suggest who he or she was. And as the tape shows the time of 3 am when he first appears, it's unlikely that anyone would have been awake to see him from inside the house.'

'Only this person,' said Sasha.

'Sorry?'

'The only one awake is the person who went in through the servant's entrance about 15 minutes before the killer.'

'Show me,' snapped Jo, wondering why Sasha had only just told them this nugget of information. But again there was nothing on the CCTV to suggest who the person was. They just got an impression of a small adult, who could have been male or female.

'His or her entry is about 15 minutes before our killer and then he leaves again 10 minutes afterwards.'

Jo had seen enough. 'Right then, Jill and Eddie, back to the house. Interview all the staff again. Try and find the insider who facilitated this. Even if you can't identify the person just yet, it could rattle his or her enough to make a stupid move and give us some sort of clue. Sasha, how are you doing with the laptops?'

'I've identified which machine belonged to which of our

victims. At the moment there's nothing incriminating, but I've yet to go into their finances via the online banking system and of course there's always any hidden files.'

'Hidden files?' said Jill.

'Oh I forgot you don't know anything about computers, Jill,' Sasha said, bluntly but not unkindly. It was just her usual way of stating the obvious. At least obvious to her if not to anyone else. Still it made Jill blush. 'Let's just say there's a system for creating files and then hiding them from any other user of the laptop. I'm hoping to find some of those, that's all. If there are any, they could give us clues as to what their crimes were that the BNL felt they needed to die for,' and Sasha turned back to her monitor and keyboard and carried on working.

Jill said a rather feeble, 'Thanks, Sasha.'

'Come on,' said Byrd, 'grab your stuff and let's get going. Let's see who we can put through the wringer.'

'Uniforms are still up there,' Jo heard Jill say as they left the offices. 'We can get them to round up the staff for us.'

When Jill and Byrd had gone, Jo looked at Sasha, hiding behind her hair as usual. It was as if she was happy blending into the background, then she'd be overlooked. Left alone. Not be forced to interact with the others.

'Sasha?' Jo said.

'Mmm,' came the reply.

'Are you enjoying working with us?'

Still hiding, Sasha nodded.

'Want to stay, do you?'

Sasha nodded, but still didn't look at Jo. Not once. Not even a peek.

'Good. We'd like you to stay too.'

'You would?'

'Sure.'

'You're not pretending so you can make fun of me?' Sasha did look at Jo then but still with her head bent downwards.

'Whatever made you say that?' Then Jo realised that

Sasha must have been bullied at school and quite possibly in previous jobs. 'No, I'm not pretending.'

'Thank you,' Sasha whispered and once more her fingers started flying over her keyboard.

Jo gathered that was the end of the conversation. She'd get in touch with HR and make Sasha's temporary appointment permanent. The girl had done a good job. It mustn't have been easy filling in for Judith. But Sasha brought her own strengths and skills to the party. She was hard working, bloody good with computers and never complained. Not once. Okay so she was a bit literal, had extreme difficulty making eye contact, but hey, everyone had their quirks and Jo had to admit that she herself had more than anyone.

57

Jo's mobile rang. She paused. She'd started not wanting to look at her mobile when it rang, in case it was Crooks. Which was ridiculous, of course. She mentally shook herself and grabbed it. The caller display told her it was her father.

'Hey, Dad,'

'Hi, just ringing to see if you fancied a coffee?'

'Now? During a workday?' she teased.

'Can't think of a better time,' he laughed.

'Where are you?'

'Right outside, Jo, right outside.'

'Hold on, I'm coming.'

Jo grabbed her bag and hurried down the stairs. As she left the station and the door swung closed behind her, her dad walked over, and they hugged.

'Wow, dad, not seen you for ages.'

'I know, this morning seems a long time ago. Come on, let's go just around the corner. I fancy sitting in the sun.'

Once settled, outside a café, she said, 'Right, what's this all about?'

'I've sensed that something's bothering you about this investigation. So spit it out. What's the problem?'

Jo gave him a watery smile. 'Which one?'

He looked at her without speaking for a moment, then

said, 'Okay, how about the biggest.'

'One word will do for that, Odin.'

'I guessed as much.'

'I just feel so impotent. I have to do something about him, before more people die. But what?'

'You'll have to confront him.'

'How? We don't know who he is, or where he is.'

He thought for a moment. 'Alex Crooks is the key then.'

'I thought you'd say that, but I'm doing a good job of keeping out of his way.'

'Looks like you'll have to try a different strategy.'

'You mean push for a meeting with Odin, don't you?'

He nodded. 'Or go along with any suggestions he might have for meeting him.'

'Crooks or Odin?'

'Probably both.'

'I don't trust him, Dad.'

'No, I know, but he could be your only way to Odin.'

Jo nodded. 'And what if I do meet Odin? What then?'

'Confront him.'

Her father made it sound so easy, but the very thought of it gave her heart palpitations. 'I can't take him on, I'm not powerful. I just see the dead. I don't have anything to take him down with. That's reckless talk. I expected better from you, Dad.'

Jo was so cross, she started to pack away her things and went to leave. Mick stopped her, grabbing hold of her arm.

'Who said you have to take him on, on your own? Trust in Judith,' he said, before Jo shook off his hand and stalked off. She'd never heard such twaddle from her father. Trust in Judith? Ha! Judith was bloody dead and gone, or didn't he get that? Walking quickly back to the station, she wiped the tears off her face. She missed Judith every minute of every day. How dare Mick be so cruel. She'd expected better of him.

58

Upon arriving at Putnam House, Byrd and Sandy had a chat with Mrs T in the kitchen. Byrd reckoned she was a safe bet. She'd been with the family for years and clearly doted on the children. Over a cup of tea and sat around the warmth of the Aga, she took them through the staff. There were a couple of cooks who lived in. Two permanent cleaners, again who lived in. Three permanent gardeners, but they didn't live on site. Two jockeys who lived above the stable block but had access to the staff entrance of the main house, of course, although one of them was on holiday, gone back to see his parents in Wales. She had a full staff list in her office, and she left them eating a particularly delicious piece of treacle cake while she printed off a copy.

Upon her return with the piece of paper detailing the staff and all their contact details, Byrd said, 'Thanks Mrs T. I didn't realise you had a computer here.'

'Oh yes, the master upgraded all the old ones, bulky things they were, and got me a laptop, one for him and one for the mistress.'

'We have those two,' Byrd said, 'but I'm afraid we're going to have to take yours as well.'

Mrs T nodded. 'I expected as much,' she said.

'Do you know what the staff were up to, the night Mr

160

and Mrs Prendergast died?'

'Let me think. Um, everyone was here, apart from the stable lad I've told you about. Oh, yes, come to think of it, Ricky, the other jockey, was up all night with that poor mare that had colic. So I guess he was out and about that night, but he's a lovely lad, I'm sure he'd not have anything to do with this nasty business.'

Jill noticed Mrs T couldn't bring herself to say the word 'murder'. She wondered what would become of all of them and the house now the couple were dead. She hoped Oliver and Olivia could keep the place going, but they were still so young and inexperienced. It was certainly a responsibility Jill wouldn't want.

Byrd drained his cup and said, 'Right, Jill, we best get on, thanks a lot for the tea and cake Mrs T.'

'Where are we off to, Boss?'

'Oh I think the stables, don't you? This Ricky sounds very interesting.'

Ricky Conran, the jockey who exercised the horses, was easy to find. He was grooming one of them in its stable when they walked up.

After introducing themselves and asking about his movements the night the murders had taken place, Conran said he was up all night with a horse that had colic, just as Mrs T had said. He clarified that it had been his job to make sure the horse kept on its feet and didn't lie down. If it did, it had a good chance of dying, apparently, and as it was a thoroughbred brood mare, that couldn't be allowed to happen. He said he'd never left the stable block that night. Had no reason to.

Eddie and Jill walked through the stables looking at the horses, the air filled with straw dust, warm from the animal's breath. Jill didn't know much about horses, but she was impressed with the animals. In the last box was a truly handsome beast. Jet black with a haughty expression, he was eyeing them. Jill thought it looked like he was trying to work them out. Friend or foe? His name plate said, 'Hercules'. He must have found something about them not to his liking for he suddenly reared up, snorting and neighing, hooves banging against the stable door. Jill back peddled, startled by the beast. Ricky poked his head out of the stable of the horse he was working on.

'Best be careful of him,' he called. 'That's Olivia's stallion. He's short tempered that one.'

'Isn't he just,' said Jill, as Hercules continued to rear up at her. She decided to take Ricky's advice. She followed Byrd out of the stable block.

'What do you reckon?' she asked him.

'Shifty little bugger, isn't he?' said Eddie. 'I reckon he's the obvious choice. I'm going to ring Sasha to see if there's any CCTV showing that he left the stable block that night.'

'Wouldn't he have been wary of the cameras?'

'Yeah, normally, but that wouldn't have been a normal night, would it? It's possible he forgot about them. He must have been in quite a state. Letting an intruder into the house at 3 am isn't normal behaviour.'

As Eddie phoned Sasha and asked her to have a look at any video from the stable block around the time their suspect entered the house through the servant's entrance, Jill returned to Ricky. Leaning over the stable door where he was working, she asked him about the horses, and what it was like working in a big house that was open to the public. Did the public come to the stables? Just general chit chat. She worked into the conversation the rise in popularity of the BNL and said that she could understand where they were coming from, especially when you saw privileged people like this lot.

'Can you?' his face became animated. 'Because I do too. It's the little people that get squashed, you know. Or kicked out of the way by the hoity-toity. I mean look at here, a private stables just for one girl. With six horses in it! And her away at University, even though she hasn't got two brain cells to rub together?' He continued grooming the mare, the muscles straining in his arms and sweat starting to gather around his hairline.

Jill stifled a giggle. 'I know what you mean,' she replied. 'And these people end up in positions of power, corrupt as hell and no one says anything. Criminal, that's what it is.'

'Yeah too right. Look,' he sidled up to her, 'if you fancy coming to a meeting, just let me know and you can come with me. What do you reckon?'

'Nice one,' said Jill. 'I'd really like that. Here,' and she slipped one of her cards into the breast pocket of his shirt. 'That's got my personal mobile number on it. Give me a ring sometime, yeah?'

'Sounds good, like. I'll be in touch,' and he winked conspiratorially as Byrd came back from talking to Sasha on the phone.

'All good here?' he asked Jill.

'Yes, Boss, no worries.'

'Good,' Byrd looked at his watch. 'We better be off then. Thanks for talking to us, Ricky, appreciate your co-operation.'

Jill and Byrd walked back towards the big house. 'Well?' he asked when they were out of earshot.

'I reckon it's him, Boss. He just offered to take me to a British Nordic League meeting.'

'Well done, Jill. I'll get a couple of uniforms over here and we'll arrest him. Let's see what he's got to say for himself once we get him back to the station. By then Sasha will have had a chance to go through the CCTV recordings again and pulled some stills that we can use.'

As Jill hurried alongside Byrd, she was ever so slightly euphoric. She didn't half love her job.

59

Leaving Ricky stewing in a cell, Byrd and Jill returned to the office to brief Jo and Sasha. Byrd let Jill tell them about her conversation with Ricky.

'So where is he now?' Jo asked.

'Downstairs waiting on a free solicitor. Says he won't speak to us without one.'

'Fair enough, that gives us some time. Sasha, any luck with your research into the Prendergast's finances?'

Sasha nodded. 'There's definitely something off here,' she said. 'But I'm not finished yet. I need to double check a few things.'

'Forget that,' said Jo. 'What have you got so far?'

Sasha huffed. She was clearly unimpressed. 'But I haven't finished,' she protested.

'I know that, Sasha, but tell me what you have so far, please.'

Byrd could see Jo wasn't going to let that one go and hoped Sasha would see sense. To help her along he explained, 'The reason the Boss wants what you have so far is that it will help with our interview with Ricky. We can't wait until tomorrow; we need something to confront him with now. It's not about you personally, and all about the investigation.'

Sasha looked up at Byrd through her curtain of hair.

'Oh alright. I found some payments that I couldn't find corresponding invoices or receipts for. They were just marked with the children's names. But there were no respective payments into the kid's accounts.'

'Who were they to?' Jill asked.

'Don't interrupt me. I'm getting to that,' Sasha snapped.

At a stare from Byrd, Jill mumbled, 'Sorry, Sasha.'

'I tracked the payments through a dummy company to the 'social and culture fund' of Portsmouth Uni.'

Jo nodded. 'So they bribed the university to take Oliver and Olivia.'

'I think so. There are also other payments that I haven't finished with yet.'

'What do you suspect they are for?'

'I don't do suspecting. I do fact.'

'I know that, Sasha, but just this once, speculate for me, will you?'

Byrd nodded his encouragement. He could see that this was an anathema for Sasha, she was fighting with herself to provide the information Jo wanted.

'It's my theory that they bribed the university to take Oliver and Oliva as you said, Jo. But I think they also had the grades on their A levels changed. I also think it could just be the tip of the iceberg.'

'Really?'

Sasha nodded. 'I think this could be part of a wider fraudulent scheme.'

'Wider?' asked Jill.

'Wider, deeper, however you want to describe it. But I don't think the Prendergast's were the only ones doing it. It looks as though there is a company who organised bribes to exam administrators and arranged the nomination of unqualified applicants to universities. I suspect this is being run as a charitable organisation to conceal the source and nature of laundered bribery payments.'

'Why a charitable organisation?' asked Jo.

'Because payments made to a non-profit organisation that has been granted charitable status, helps in two ways. Firstly the charities avoid income tax on the payments they receive, and secondly the parents are able to deduct the donations from their own personal taxes.'

Byrd whistled. 'Jesus, Sasha,' he said. 'Do you think you're right about this?' Sasha lifted her head and stared at Byrd. Actually stared. 'I guess you do.'

'Good work, Sasha,' said Jo.

'But like I said, I've not finished yet. At the moment it's a… a… working theory,' she finished with a flourish.

60

Ricky sat sullenly in the interview room. He looked dusty and had bits of straw caught in his clothes and his hair. He didn't smell very nice either. Jo figured that at some point that morning he'd been mucking out the stables.

'What's this all about?' he snapped. 'You've no right to keep me here.' He stopped talking as the solicitor put a hand on his shoulder.

'As you know, Mr and Mrs Prendergast were murdered. In their beds. In the middle of the night,' said Jo.

'So?'

'So we've been looking at the staff to find who might hate them enough to carry out the killings.'

'I never killed nobody.'

'Oh, so you did?'

'What? No, I never.'

'You see the thing is, Ricky, double negatives cancel each other out.'

'What?'

'If you say, 'no I never', then you must mean that you did.'

'What?'

Byrd grinned. Ricky was becoming stressed, wrong footed, which is how Jo wanted him to be.

'It must have been an inside job,' continued Jo. 'There was no evidence of a break in and the alarms were still on when the housekeeper got up that morning.'

'So?'

'So, we saw an intruder on the CCTV system.'

'The what?'

'CCTV. The whole estate has cameras on it.'

Ricky didn't say anything, but Byrd noticed he'd gone pale.

'The intruder was let into the house, Ricky. We saw it.'

The young man started chewing his nails.

'Did you let him in?'

Now his leg was jiggling up and down.

'See we think you did.'

'No, I never, I've told you that.'

There was perspiration blossoming on his top lip.

'But we have you on CCTV going to the house in the middle of the night. You let yourself in, using your key. Five minutes later, you opened the door and let the intruder in. See, the thing is, we believe you then joined the intruder in killing Mr and Mrs Prendergast as they slept in their beds. And the reason was because the BNL had found out that the Prendergasts were paying bribes to get their children into Portsmouth University. So you were instructed to kill them.'

'No. No, I never did!'

This time his solicitor interrupted. 'I'd like a few minutes alone with my client, please.'

Jo and Byrd looked at each other. Jo nodded and they left the room after suspending the interview.

Fifteen minutes later they were back.

Ricky didn't speak. Just his solicitor. 'My client is prepared to admit that he let the intruder into the house. But he had no idea why the man was there, or what he was about to do.'

Byrd snorted.

'So in return for a lesser charge, he's prepared to admit that he was acting on the instructions of the British Nordic League.'

Byrd smiled sardonically.

'On who's orders?' Jo asked.

'Odin's.'

Now there was something they could work with.

61

Jo was in her office, reading through the transcripts of Ricky's interviews when DCI Crooks called in.

'Sir,' Jo said and stood as he entered.

He waived her down.

'I just thought I'd pop in for an update, as I was passing,' he said.

Jo wasn't sure she believed him. She'd managed to successfully avoid him as much as possible lately. This visit was more to pin her down, rather than anything else, she was sure.

'We've just finished interviewing a suspect in the Prendergast killings,' she said and went on to tell Alex about Ricky's admission that he was working on the orders of Odin. 'But he doesn't know who he let in as they were wearing one of those masks.'

Jo knew she was looking pretty smug.

When Alex didn't speak, she continued, 'Also, Sasha thinks the Prendergasts were knee deep in muck and not just from the stables. She is pretty sure they were part of a conspiracy to defraud the university about Olivia and Oliver's grades, to facilitate their entry. We'll be passing everything we've got on that over to the Fraud Squad.'

'And the post-mortem?' Alex asked. 'Any results yet?'

'Yes, Jeremy has just sent through the post-mortem results. He's firmly of the opinion that Mr and Mrs Prendergast must have been subdued first, probably from something like chloroform. That's because there was no sign of a struggle at the scene, nor any signs of a struggle on their bodies and there were small pieces of lint in their airways. They both seemed to have passively lain there and bled out. The cuts to their necks were caused by a very sharp, thin blade. He thought it was a professional job as there were no hesitation cuts.'

Jo thought Alex looked shocked by her revelations. But didn't understand why. Her team had found the insider who had helped kill the Prendergasts and uncovered the reason that Odin wanted them dead. What was there to be shocked about? They were good at their job.

Crooks mumbled, 'Good work, Jo,' then left. No more praise than that. No emotional blackmail of Jo. No unwanted advances. Oh well, her lucky day, she thought as he left her office. She watched his progress through the floor. He was definitely off. Ignoring everyone, looking at no one. Oh well, at least he'd left her alone. Thank goodness for small mercies.

***

Alex finally reached his office pale and shaken by Jo's news. He never thought they'd make the connection so quickly. Bloody Ricky. Alex had told Odin he didn't think Ricky was strong enough to carry out such a vital role without breaking. And it turned out that he had been right, although that gave him no satisfaction. The boy was simply too young and, to be honest, too thick. Fancy boasting to Jill about being part of the BNL and offering to take her to a meeting. Jesus.

And so now he had a personal dilemma. Should he stay quiet or tell Odin what had just happened. Alex quickly decided that he needed to warn Odin. The man was his leader, his lover, his life. Of course he'd choose Odin over the police force. Pulling out his keys from his trouser pocket, Alex unlocked a drawer in his desk, removing a burner phone with just one number on it. He ambled from his office and headed for the lifts. Once in the foyer he left the building, walking out into the sunny but blustery day. He headed towards the Cathedral gardens to send his message. He was so focused he didn't look up. If he had have done, he would have seen Jo watching him from the window in her office.

62

Alex sat on a bench, turning the phone over and over in his hand. He had sent a message requesting a meeting with Odin, then deleted it. As he waited for a reply, he looked around him. No one else was sat down, it was too cold a day for it he guessed, as a particularly cold gust of wind blew around him, managing to burrow its way through the thickness of his jacket. He looked at the phone, a small black handset, as cheap as chips. He hoped the reply would come through soon and he stuffed the phone in his pocket along with his hands. He was just thinking that perhaps he should go and get a take-away coffee, when his pocket buzzed.

With bumbling hands, he pulled the phone out, flipped it open and read the message. It simply informed him of a date, time and location. He then deleted that message also. He appreciated the need for secrecy. His colleagues in the police mustn't know what he was up to. That he was, in essence, a double agent, working for the police, but essentially Odin's man. The police thought he was infiltrating the British Nordic League for them and was dutifully relaying information on the inner workings of the fascist group. Most of what he had told them was rubbish, designed to throw the police off the scent. He was making up meetings with Odin's leadership team and recounting experiences at BNL rallies, which had very little to do with real life and were worthy of any novelist.

However, this meeting was very real and due to take place that night at midnight.

Somehow Alex got through the day, mostly by hiding in his office and pretending to work. He couldn't eat that night and ended up throwing his supper in the bin. He was tempted by a glass of wine, but again managed to push it away, undrunk. After staring, unseeing, at the television, it was finally time for him to leave the house. He walked to a local park a few hundred yards away and was collected from there by a black Land Rover Discovery. Once inside the car he was driven to a secret location. It was secret because Alex had no idea where it was. After being greeted by the bull-headed bouncer, whose name Alex still didn't know, he was blindfolded.

When the blindfold was taken off, he appeared to be in a large warehouse with a small office in the corner. Alex was pushed forward by his minders towards the office and opened the door. He was an emotional mess by then. He'd waited all day and most of the night for this. Excitement fizzed in his blood and he hoped to have some time with Odin alone. Their previous meetings had been snatched moments. Alex understood the reason for this, after all Odin was very busy, but he was desperate to bask in his God's glory. He likened it to a drug addict. First came the sweet anticipation, then the buzz of the high, finally the comedown, which once again turned into anticipation.

Odin was stood with his back to the door and when he turned Alex gasped. He couldn't help himself. The man shimmered in front of him. He was there but wasn't there. A contradiction in terms, certainly, and Alex was having difficulty getting his head around it. It was almost as if Odin was a hologram, just like in a science fiction movie. If Alex reached out his hand, he was sure it would pass straight through Odin. It was outside Alex's experience or understanding, but he wasn't frightened, merely fascinated.

However, the man's charisma wasn't diminished by not having a physical presence. Alex was in awe of the God who was within an arm's length of him. He told Odin about the fallout from the Prendergast murders and how well Jo and her team were doing. He confirmed that Ricky was in custody and about to be charged with conspiracy to murder. The breakthrough had come because DC Jill Sandy had been invited to a British Nordic League meeting by the unfortunate stable hand. Ricky was now a liability.

After a moment or two, Odin spoke softly and persuasively, making Alex shiver with desire and ecstasy. Odin was walking around him, weaving his spell. Alex could feel the breath on his ear and neck, as Odin whispered to him, sending frissons of desire through him. Alex still couldn't believe that the wonderful God, Odin, was interested in him. Not even his wife had made him feel this proud, this desirable, this wanted and needed.

Odin outlined his plan to Alex, but first, swore him to secrecy. No one must be alerted about what was going to happen, otherwise the plan would fail, and Odin didn't do failure as Ricky would soon find out to his detriment. Odin also told him about the wonderful future Alex could have with the organisation, once this particularly unfortunate matter was dealt with. Odin was looking forward to a continued close relationship with Alex, who would rise further up the ranks of the police force, maximising his use to the party.

The thought of the power he would wield almost made Alex swoon. The more power Alex had, the more use he would be to Odin, which in turn meant a closer relationship with him.

All too soon Alex was told to leave and to make the arrangements for the plan, as soon as possible. Alex left the office reluctantly, wishing he had more time with Odin. He just wanted to be near to the man, to be bathed in the light that surrounded him. Alex could feel the God's power and love he had for his organisation and followers. To be part of that meant far more to Alex than the police force ever had.

As Alex walked across the warehouse to be taken back home, the light went out in the small office. But Alex didn't notice, he was still enjoying the sensation of being close to Odin and having his ear and his trust. Yes, the meeting confirmed Crooks' feeling that he had done the right thing by telling Odin what was going on with the Prendergast investigation. He'd told Odin who was in charge of the case and he had been given his instructions.

He must take Jo to meet Odin.

63

Crooks wasted no time and accosted Jo as she was leaving work the next day. He was already waiting by her car when she arrived. 'Ah, Jo, there you are,' he said.

'Boss?' Jo's heart sank. Was Alex back on the full charm offensive? She bloody well hoped not.

Alex looked around to make sure they weren't being observed. 'I've finally got a meeting with Odin. And I want you to come with me.'

'Me?'

'Yes, but only you.'

'Why? Why just you and me?'

'Because we're the ones that deserve the arrest. I've put my life on the line multiple times for the force and I don't want anyone fucking it up. I need you with me. I trust you to have my back. No one else.'

Jo was appalled. 'Boss, this is madness!'

'Look, just be there for me, that's all I ask. How can you not after all we've meant to each other?' Alex implored.

Jo chewed the inside of her cheek. She thought what Alex was doing was reckless, and that he was exaggerating their working and personal relationship, but if she couldn't persuade him not to go, neither could she leave him to go on his own. As far as she knew this was the first time Alex had met Odin, so he was naturally reluctant to go alone. Although he was begging her, she could also see the steely determination in his eyes. He'd decided this meeting would happen and that Jo would go with him. He wouldn't want to miss this opportunity and really who could blame him.

'Very well, Boss,' she said reluctantly. 'Let me know when and where it is. I'd like to suss out the meeting place before we go in. Make sure there are no surprises, nowhere where Odin could have backup hidden. And we'll need armed police. Perhaps even be armed ourselves. We'll be facing a criminal responsible for the death of many lives and I want us to have all the advantages possible.'

'Sorry, that's not going to happen.'

'What do you mean?' Jo took a step back. 'This operation has to be carefully planned. It won't work otherwise.' Jo folded her arms. The back of her neck was prickling, and hairs were standing up on her forearms. She didn't like this one little bit. Perhaps she should go back into the building and tell the Assistant Chief Constable that Alex was acting in a reckless manner that could get members of her team killed. But could she really go above her boss and report him? What opinion would the ACC have of her after that? Would he see her as a woman who couldn't follow orders? Or a woman who cared enough to help stop her superior officer making the worst decision of his career? But in the end, she didn't have the opportunity to do any of that.

'We're going now, Jo.'

'Now? No, Alex this is madness,' she grabbed his arm. 'You can't be serious.'

'Now, now, Jo, don't panic, it's going to be fine, you must trust me. I've never put you in danger before, have I?'

Alex put his hand on Jo's back and steered her towards his car, without waiting for an answer to his rhetorical question. Opening the door for her he helped her in. She was still in shock. This couldn't be happening. But there didn't seem to be anything she could do that would stop it. She could get out of the car. But then she'd be abandoning

Crooks to his fate. She couldn't do that either. Wouldn't do that to any of her colleagues. She had to have Alex's back. Jo swore under her breath but decided to do as Crooks asked. She couldn't think of any alternative.

***

Byrd stood at the window in the stairwell, overlooking the car park. He'd been about to run after Jo and suggest they got a Chinese take-away that night, when he saw Crooks approach her. They had an animated conversation, with Crooks' hands all over Jo, which was bad enough, but then as Byrd watched, Crooks put his hand on Jo's back and persuaded her into his car.

Byrd clenched his fist in anger. He was holding his car keys which were digging into his palm, but he ignored the pain. As Crooks climbed into the driver's seat, Byrd made a decision. He turned and ran down the remaining stairs. Fuck it. He was going to follow them to find out what the hell was going on. Jo had kept telling him that there was nothing to her relationship with Alex Crooks. That they weren't having an affair. That it was one sided. Not reciprocated. But he wasn't sure Alex felt the same way, as Byrd was convinced Alex still harboured feelings for Jo. Byrd needed to see for himself what was actually going on. Perhaps it was his natural curiosity, being a policeman. He needed evidence that Jo was telling the truth.

As he reached his car, he saw Crooks drive to the car park's exit and turn left. It didn't take long for Byrd to climb in and follow them.

64

This time Crooks knew what he was doing and where he was going. No longer had he to go to see Odin blindfolded but had been given precise instructions as to the location for the meeting. He drove North, away from the city centre. As he drove, the landscape became more and more isolated and desolate.

'Where are we going, Alex?' Jo kept asking, but he wouldn't tell her.

'We'll be there soon.'

And then they were.

Alex pulled up alongside a cavernous warehouse, the same one that he'd visited the night before. There was no evidence of any other followers, or protectors. Crooks found that strange, there had always been others around Odin when Alex had seen him. He tried not to look perturbed.

'Alex, what the hell is going on?'

'There's to be a BNL meeting here.'

'When?'

'Now.'

'But there's no one here.'

They both got out of the car and Alex couldn't hear anything but the wind whistling along the dusty fields.

'I think someone has been pulling your leg, Alex, there's no meeting here. If there was there would be cars, noise, people.' Then she spoke the words he didn't want to hear. 'This could be a set-up, Alex. I think we should leave.'

'Don't be silly,' he told her. 'Come on, let's investigate. That's what policemen do, isn't it?'

He'd tried for humour, but it hadn't worked. By the look on Jo's face, she was furious with him. But she wouldn't be soon. She'd be as besotted by Odin as he was. Just like everyone else who met him was. He shut the car door and hurried to the small door set in the side of the warehouse. He felt like a child at Christmas, eager to get downstairs and see the wonderful treats Santa had left for him.

***

Byrd, however, was having none of those feelings. He'd followed Crooks and Jo out of the city, falling further back as they'd traversed the industrial centre and arrived at a large, barren area. Byrd recognised it as one of the old farms that had gone bankrupt. This was part of the building plot that had been earmarked by Truelove for his dodgy scheme. The bomb at the restaurant sometimes seemed long ago, and at others as though it had happened only yesterday. Byrd guessed he was still coming to terms with the horror of it and the loss of Judith.

Eddie parked his car against the other side of the warehouse and tentatively walked along the back of it, peering round the edge. He saw first Alex Crooks and then Jo enter the building. They hadn't seen him. So far so good. But he had no idea at all what he was going to be facing inside. No idea if there would be anywhere to hide.

Fuck it. He had to go after Jo. He couldn't leave her to face whatever it was inside the warehouse alone. He didn't trust Crooks as far as he could throw him, as the saying went. So he had no choice. He followed them in.

65

The inside of the warehouse housed old, unused farm equipment. The beams above them sagged and bagged, dripping in cobwebs and rust. Pigeons could be heard cooing from the rafters. Old, rotting, tarpaulins were strewn around, and the odd hay bale peppered the ground like tumbleweed. The air smelled musty. They'd left the entrance door open, but the late afternoon sunlight failed to penetrate far enough for Jo to see all of the space and there were malevolent shadows collecting at the far end.

It was from one of those shadows that a man appeared and started to walk towards them. Because of the bad light, Jo couldn't make out the man's features, but golden curls sprang from his head and moved around as though with a life of their own. He was well built, solid and muscular and exuded power. His movements were haughty and regal. He was taller than them and dominated the space. Jo was in no doubt that she was in the presence of Odin.

Alex started to gabble. Explaining that he'd brought Jo to Odin as requested. He started fawning, practically bowing and scraping. Alex was treating the man as though he were a god, a deity, someone to be worshiped and adored. Jo had never seen Alex like this before. This powerful police chief inspector reduced to a mere hanger-on. Jo was horrified.

'Alex,' she cried. 'What the hell's going on?'

'It's alright,' he replied tearing his eyes from Odin and looking at her. But they didn't stay on her for long. His focus kept being drawn back to Odin. 'Odin just wanted to meet you, didn't you, Odin? Just so he could explain his vision to you. I'm sure once you hear what he's got to say you'll be convinced too. You'll want to join the BNL. Won't she, Odin?'

'Shut up.'

The harshness in Odin's voice stopped Alex's gabbling. But it seemed he couldn't keep quiet for long. 'It would be wonderful, Jo, for us to be together, both serving Odin.'

'Alex…' Odin rumbled, the warning heard by Jo, but ignored by Alex.

'Just think of the life we could have…'

Odin raised his arm and pointed his finger at Alex. Jo watched on helpless as a crackle of lightening appeared from it, jumping across the space and hitting Alex squarely on the forehead. Alex's head shot backwards and Odin moved his arm downward, this time his finger pointing at Alex's chest.

'No!' shouted Jo.

The only response was laughter as Odin continued to hit Alex with bolt after bolt of lightning. As the air became charged with electricity, Alex's eyes bulged, his tongue swelled and burst. Smoke was coming from his hair, before bursting into flames. His body jumped around like a marionette, lifting clear of the floor, before Odin dropped his arm. Then the lightening drained out of Alex and he landed on the ground with a thump. Discordant twitching continued, before finally Alex stilled. Jo ran to his side and felt the side of Alex's neck, but there was nothing. No welcome pulse beating under her fingers. His body was already cooling. There was nothing Jo could do for him.

She stood, 'You bastard,' she raged. 'Alex didn't deserve that!'

Odin laughed. 'Yes, he did, he was a wimp and a

sycophant. His only mission was to bring you to me and as he'd achieved that, he was of no more use. You, on the other hand, are much more valuable. I have great plans for us.'

66

'You must have me mistaken for someone else,' Jo told Odin, squaring up to him. 'There is nothing you can say to me that would persuade me to join you and your organisation. You are the antithesis of everything I stand for.'

'Is that right?' Odin smiled.

It was like the sun coming out on a cloudy day. That smile. Jo started to relax. Her mind wanted to bask in its warmth. Then she remembered where she was. Who she was. She blinked and took a deep breath, trying to steel herself against Odin. To build a barrier in her mind against him.

'You have a lover, don't you, Jo?' Odin asked, taking a step towards her. 'DS Byrd, I believe.'

Jo found herself nodding.

'Perhaps he'd like to join us as well? Wouldn't that be wonderful?'

Jo had to admit that it would be. 'Yes,' she whispered. She felt her body beginning to relax. Images of Byrd went through her mind. With each one, she melted a little more. She was just about to relive one of their lingering kisses when a voice inside her head said, *'Jo, don't listen to him.'*

'What?'

'Don't listen to him, he's evil. He's trying to bend your mind. You must resist.'

'But he has Byrd! Leave me alone! I have to join Byrd.'

'He doesn't have Byrd, Jo, you must believe me!'

Jo knew she'd heard that voice before… Judith! It was Judith!

'Fight him, Jo.'

'But I can't, Judith, not on my own. He's too strong.'

'You're not on your own. I'll prove it. But first you must have faith in me. Trust me, Jo.'

Jo did trust Judith. She always had. Her father's words echoed in her head. Trust in Judith. And so Jo pulled at the cobwebs in her mind, tore them down, banished the pictures of Eddie that Odin had placed there.

'It won't work, Odin,' she said. 'It will never work. I won't join you.' As she said the words, Jo believed them more and more. She stood up straight, squared her shoulders as though she were in the army and on parade.

'Ha!' he scoffed. 'You can't beat me. If you won't join me, I'll destroy you. Then you'll never see your precious Byrd again. Is that what you want, Jo?'

Jo stood resolute.

'Very well. It's your death.'

Odin raised his arm.

Oh, shit, Jo thought. Here goes nothing. And so she also raised her arm, aiming her palm squarely at Odin's head.

'It's you that needs to leave, Odin,' she ordered. 'Walk away now, otherwise you will be destroyed. The choice is yours.'

He laughed at her again asking, 'What the hell can you do on your own?'

'But I'm not on my own,' said Jo as Judith appeared at Jo's shoulder.

Clearly flustered, Odin spat, 'How the hell did you do that? You are a mere human. I am a spirit. A God. You can't defeat me!'

'You are an evil spirit and goodness will defeat you.'

But instead of turning and running, all Odin did was to laugh in Jo's face.

'In that case you're a braver man than me,' said Jo.

67

One by one they appeared, the dead from the restaurant. Jo didn't need to turn around to look at them. She could feel their presence and hear their words.

Mateo, the maître d'. 'You took my life, left my wife a widow and my children fatherless. I'll never forgive you for that.'

Tony, the chef. 'How dare you take my precious restaurant. I was happy there. I poured all my heart into those dishes. I'll never forgive you for that.'

Paul the commis chef. 'I had my whole life before me. Years and years of happiness. My parents will never recover from their loss. I'll never forgive you for that.'

Nick, the pot wash. 'I had nothing. Then Tony believed in me and gave me a job. After years of being homeless on the streets, he held out the hand of friendship. Then you killed us and took away my future. I'll never forgive you for that.'

Truelove the dodgy MP spat at him. 'I thought I was bad, but you are pure evil. I did what I did for money, but I never killed anyone. I'll never forgive you for all the lives you've taken.'

Truelove's wife. 'What did I ever do to you? I didn't know about my husband's dodgy dealings. But he didn't need to die for them and neither did I, nor my unborn child. I'll never forgive you for that.'

The remaining dead spoke all at once; John Jenkins, Harold Smith, Stephen McGrath, Lord Holland, Judge Chambers, Mr and

Mrs Prendergast.

Finally, Alex's spirit lifted from his body and joined them. 'I loved you and you took my love and threw it away like it was a piece of rubbish. I meant nothing to you. I'll never forgive you for that.'

Jo finally realised that individually they could never defeat Odin, not even be a speck of dust in his eye. But together, that was a different thing. As they each confronted Odin with his evil and refused to pardon him for his sins against them, it was as though he was being pummelled one by one. They all had raised hands and Jo could see and feel the power coming from them. And it was all focused on Odin. Their combined power took Odin to his knees. Odin raised his head and screamed out his anger and hatred of them. But it wasn't enough.

With a clap of thunder, he splintered, the broken, jagged pieces of him suspended in the air for a moment. In one, Jo saw his face, surprise and agony written across it, in another his slashed and burned torso, then one with arms and legs broken and bleeding. For one blinding moment they fused back together before finally turning into a single bolt of lightning that struck the ground and then burned out, never to be seen again. The God of War had fought his final battle and been found wanting.

They had used the definition of fascism against him. Jo remembered Byrd saying, 'Fascism is named after the fasces, which is an old Roman name for a group of sticks tied together. It is easy to break one stick in half. But it is very hard to break many sticks tied together, in half. Fascists think that everyone rigidly following the same leader and nationalist ideas and ideals, makes the country strong in the same way that the sticks are strong.'

Byrd had prophesised the downfall of Odin and their triumph without realising what he'd said.

One by one the dead faded away. The last one to go was Judith, of course, but this time instead of crying she was smiling at Jo. A beatific smile. Jo knew she wouldn't see Judith again and that was good. Judith would be at peace now.

Jo was left alone. Drained, but relieved it was all over.

But she would have to report Alex's death, his body was still lying on the floor. She squatted down, wondering how she'd explain his deformed face. But the horrendous injuries weren't there any longer. Alex was lying dead, but whole, at her feet. She expected he'd be found to have suffered a heart attack, when they came to confront Odin, who had never appeared. Odin would never be seen again and without him the British Nordic League were finished. Only Jo would know the real reason behind his disappearance, for she could never tell anyone what had happened that afternoon. Well, apart from her father that was.

Her father would be pleased it was all over, she thought. He was more worried for her than he'd said. She figured he'd been talking to Keith Thomas, who helped keep both of them sane with his support and insight. She could never thank him enough for helping to keep her safe from the power of the evil being that it had been her destiny to fight.

At last things could go back to normal. She wanted nothing more than to go home to Byrd, glad that he knew nothing of her gift, or her curse, depending on how you looked at it.

Then she heard a voice.

'Jo?'

She turned and there was Eddie, disbelief and horror exuding from him. She couldn't speak. Didn't know what to say.

'Jo, what the fuck just happened? What haven't you been telling me?'

***

Watching the Dead
Jo Wolfe, psychic detective book 3.

After Jo's last case, the dead are screaming no longer and have the peaceful rest they deserve. But can Jo get Byrd back on-side? Or does he no longer have her back?

Soon Jo is thrust back into another case. A man calling himself The Watcher is terrorising young women in Chichester. He rapes them in the hope of getting them pregnant. He leaves behind his signature at the crime scenes, pumpkins with enigmatic messages pinned to them.

The only flaw in his plan is that all the pregnant women have abortions.

Or do they?

Can there be a child born from this devil's seed?

And can Jo and Byrd find the happiness they both deserve?

This is the third in a new series following Jo Wolfe, a detective who developed psychic abilities after a riding accident. The only person who knows about her gift (or curse depending upon your point of view) is her father and together they attempt to right the wrongs of the living, with the aid of the dead.

Wendy Cartmell is well known for her bestselling, chilling crime thrillers and Sgt Major Crane mysteries. Several of them have ghostly and psychic elements and wanting to develop these themes further, she decided it was time she wrote a supernatural suspense series.

Watching the Dead is available from your local AMAZON.

Printed in Great Britain
by Amazon